Isabella M. A

Tuscan Folk-Lore and Sketches

Isabella M. Anderton

Tuscan Folk-Lore and Sketches

1st Edition | ISBN: 978-3-73408-084-5

Place of Publication: Frankfurt am Main, Germany

Year of Publication: 2019

Outlook Verlag GmbH, Germany.

TUSCAN FOLK-LORE

AND

SKETCHES

"*A Land of Cypresses and Olives*"

TUSCAN FOLK-LORE
AND SKETCHES

TOGETHER WITH SOME

OTHER PAPERS

BY

ISABELLA M. ANDERTON

Edited, with a BIOGRAPHICAL NOTE, by her brothers
H. Orsmond Anderton and Basil Anderton

London
ARNOLD FAIRBAIRNS
20 CHEAPSIDE, E.C.

1905

THE CAMPFIELD PRESS
ST. ALBANS

TUSCAN FOLK-LORE

HE following stories were told to me by various peasants during a summer stay amid the Tuscan Apennines above Pistoia. I had gone there with a companion in search of quiet for the summer holidays. But I fell ill, and, there being no nurses and no doctors, was tended by an old peasant woman, who, living alone (for her sons had married and left her), was only too glad to spend the warmth of her heart in "keeping me company" and tending me to the best of her ability. Long were the hours which she spent by my bedside, or by my hammock in the woods, knitting and telling me stories. She would take no payment for her time, for was she not born a twin-sister? and everyone knows that a twin-sister, left alone, must needs attach herself to someone else in the emptiness of her heart. So old Clementina attached herself to me as long as I stopped in that village; and when I left it she would write me, by means of the *scrivano*, long letters full of village news, and expressions of affection in the sweet poetical Tuscan tongue.

Indelibly is the remembrance of the kind hospitality of those peasants impressed on my mind. For Clementina, although my dearest, was by no means my only friend. I had to leave her as soon as I could be moved, for a village which boasted at any rate a chemist's and a butcher's; and there, in the two months of my stay, wandering about among the little farms, either alone, or in the company of a woman whose husband had sent her back for the summer to her native place, I had continual opportunities of chatting with the people and enjoying their disinterested hospitality. Such records as I have preserved I give to the public, thinking that others, too, might like to penetrate into that quiet country world, see the workings of the peasant mind in one or two of their stories, and note the curiously altered versions of childhood acquaintances or of old legends which have found their way into those remote regions: note, too, the lack of imagination, and the shrewdness visible in the tales which are indigenous. As regards style, I have endeavoured to preserve as closely as possible the old woman's diction.

A TUSCAN SNOW-WHITE AND THE DWARFS

T was old Clementina—a white-haired, delicate-featured peasant woman, with a brightly-coloured handkerchief tied cornerwise on her head, a big ball of coarse white wool stuck on a little stick in the right-hand side of the band of her big apron, and the sock she was knitting carried in the other hand. My companion had gone down to Pistoia to do some shopping: I was alone in our rooms in the straggling primitive little village that clings to the hill among the chestnut woods above. Clementina thought I must be very lonely; besides, she was anxious to know what sort of things these extraordinary "*forestieri*"—foreigners—did all by themselves. They wrote, she believed—well, but how did they look when they were writing, and what sort of tools did they use? So she suddenly appeared in the doorway with a bright smile, and:—"*Buon giorno a Lei.*" It was just lunch time, so I pushed aside my work, glad enough, as it happened, to see her; begged her to sit down and tell me while I ate, one of those nice stories which she, as great-grandmother, must know so well.

My lunch was the "*necci*" of the country people—a cake of sweet chestnut-flour cooked in leaves of the same tree and eaten with cheese—mountain strawberries, brown bread and country wine. Through the open window of the whitewashed room came the noises of the village street, the fresh mountain breeze and the bright sunlight which lighted up the old woman's well-cut features and kindling brown eyes, as, seating herself with the grace of any lady, she leaned forward and began:—

Once upon a time there lived a king who had one little girl called Elisa. She was a dear little girl, and her father and mother loved her very much. But presently her mother died, and the step-mother got quite angry with jealousy of the poor little thing. She thought and she thought what she could do to her, and at last she called a witch and said:—

"Get rid of Elisa for me."

The witch spirited her away into some meadows a long, long way off, in quite another country, and left her there all alone; so that poor little Elisa was very frightened. Presently there came by three fairies who loved her because she was so pretty, and asked her who she was. She said she was a king's daughter, but she did not know where her home was or how she had come to be where she was now, and that she was very unhappy.

"Come with us," said the fairies, "and we will take care of you."

So they led her into another field where was a big hole. They took her down into the hole, and there was the most beautiful palace that Elisa had ever seen in her life.

"This palace is yours," said the fairies, "live here, and do just as you like."

Well, time went by and Elisa forgot her home, and was very happy, when one night her step-mother had a dream. She dreamt that Elisa was not dead, but alive and happy. She called the witch again, and said:—

"Elisa is not dead, she is alive and well. Take some *schiacciata* (a kind of cake), put poison in it, and take it to her. She is very fond of *schiacciata*, and will be sure to eat it."

So the witch went to the hole and called "Elisa."

"What do you want?" said Elisa.

"Here's some *schiacciata* for you."

"I don't want *schiacciata*," said Elisa; "I have plenty."

"Well, I'll put it here, and you can take it if you like": so she put it down and went away.

Presently there came by a dog, who ate the *schiacciata* and immediately fell down dead. In the evening the fairies came home, took up the dog and showed him to Elisa.

"See you never take anything that anyone brings you," said they, "or this will happen to you, too."

Then they put the dog into their garden.

After a time the queen dreamt again that Elisa was alive and happy, so she called the witch and said:—

"Elisa is very fond of flowers; pick a bunch and cast a spell upon them, so that whoever smells them shall be bewitched."

The witch did as she was told, and took the flowers to the hole.

"Elisa," she called down.

"What is it?" said Elisa.

"Here are some flowers for you."

"Well, you can put them down and go away. I don't want them."

So the witch put them down and went home. Soon some sheep and a shepherd came by; the sheep saw the flowers, smelt them and became spell-bound; the shepherd went to drive off the sheep, and became spell-bound too. When the fairies came home that night, they found the sheep and the shepherd, showed them to Elisa as a warning, and put them too into their garden.

But the queen dreamt a third time, and a third time she called the witch, saying:—

"Elisa is well and happy. Take a pair of golden slippers this time, *pianelle* (slippers with a covering for the toe only), bewitch them, and take them to Elisa: those she will certainly put on."

And the queen was right. When the witch had gone away from the hole Elisa came up to look at the pretty golden *pianelle*. First she took them in her hands, and then she put one on, and afterwards the other. As soon as she had done it she was quite spell-bound, and could not move. When the fairies came home they were very sad. They took her up and put her into the garden, with the dog, the sheep, and the shepherd, because they did not know what else to do with her.

There she stayed a long time, till one day the king's son rode by as he went out hunting. He looked through the garden gate, and saw Elisa.

"Oh, look," said he to the hunters, "look at that lovely girl who does not move; I never saw anyone so beautiful. I must have her."

So he went into the garden, took Elisa, carried her home, and put her into a glass case in his room. Now he spent all the time in his room; he would never come out, and would not even let the servants in to make his bed, for he loved Elisa more and more every day, and could not bear to leave her, or to let anyone else see her.

"What can be in there?" said the servants; "we can't keep his room clean if we're not allowed to go into it."

So they watched their opportunity, and one day when the prince had gone to take the holy water, they made their way in to dust.

"Oh! oh!" said they, "the prince was quite wise to keep his room shut up. What a beautiful woman, and what lovely slippers!"

With that one went up, and said, "This slipper's a little dusty; I'll dust it."

While he was doing so, it moved; so he pushed it a little more, and it came off altogether. Then he took off the other too, and immediately Elisa came back to life. When the prince came home he wanted to marry her at once; but his father said:—

"How do you know who she is? She may be a beggar's daughter."

7

"Oh, no," said Elisa, "I'm a princess," and she told them her father's name.

Then a grand wedding feast was prepared, to which her father and step-mother were invited; and they came, not knowing who the bride was to be. When they saw Elisa, the father was very glad, but the step-mother was so angry that she went and hanged herself. Nevertheless the marriage feast went off merrily. Elisa and the prince were very happy, and presently united the two kingdoms under their single rule. If they're not alive now, they must be dead; and if they're not dead, they must still be alive.

MONTE ROCHETTINO

WE were in the chestnut woods; I swinging lazily in my hammock, Clementina with her knitting, sitting on the grass beside me, a pretty clear pool reflecting the trees at our feet.

"Do you know the story of Monte Rochettino?" asked Clementina, taking a piece of dry bread to keep her mouth moist.

"No," said I.

So she settled herself comfortably and began the following curious tale, in which ever and anon one seems to recognise a likeness to the old Greek legend of Cupid and Psyche; but a likeness all distorted in transmission through ignorant, unimaginative minds:—

Once upon a time there was a widow with three daughters. ("Women always have three daughters in fairy tales," she added, by way of parenthesis.) This widow was very poor, so that when a famine came over the country she and her children were almost dying with hunger, and had to go out into the fields and get grass to eat. Once as they were looking for food they found a beautiful golden cabbage. The eldest girl took a *zappa* (a sort of pickaxe with only one arm to it) and tried to root up the cabbage. This she could not succeed in doing, but she broke off a leaf which she took to the market, and sold for a hundred gold scudi.

The next day the second daughter went, worked all day at the cabbage, and broke off two leaves. Away she went with them to the market, and got two hundred gold scudi.

The third morning the youngest daughter took the *zappa*, and went into the field. At the very first stroke the whole cabbage came up, and a little man jumped out of the earth; a very tiny little man he was, but beautifully dressed. He took the maiden by the hand, and led her down a flight of stairs underground. There she found herself in a beautiful palace, such as she had never dreamt of, all golden and shining. The little man gave her a bunch of keys, and said:—

"This palace is yours, you may do what you like, and go where you like in it. You are the mistress of it. The master of it, your husband, you will not see, he will only come to you at night. Be happy, and make no effort to look at him, or you will lose everything. If you want anything in the daytime call Monte Rochettino."

With that the little man vanished. The maiden wandered all over the new dwelling, and when it was dark she laid herself down and waited for her husband, the master of the palace. So time went on. She loved her husband, although she had never seen him, and felt that she would be very happy if only she could know something about her mother and sisters.

At last she could bear the suspense no longer, and one morning she called "Monte Rochettino!"

In an instant the little man stood before her.

"Oh, Monte Rochettino," said she, "let me go home and see my mother and sisters. Poor things, they must be so sad at losing me; they'll think I am dead."

"You'll betray me," said Monte Rochettino.

"No, no, I won't: I promise you: only let me just go and see them."

"Well, go, but be sure you don't betray me, and be back in three days."

So the girl went home, and her mother and sisters did all they could to prove their joy at seeing her, poor things. Then they asked her where she lived, and she told them she lived with her husband in a beautiful palace underground; but that her husband came to her at night, and she had never seen him. Then her mother said to her:—

"I will give you these matches and this candle. When he is asleep, light the candle, and see what he has round his neck."

So the girl took the matches and the candle and went back to the palace.

"Well, have you betrayed me?" said Monte Rochettino.

"No," said she.

"The better for you," answered the little man.

That night while her husband was asleep, the girl got up softly, lighted the candle, and saw a box round her husband's neck. The key was in the lock, she turned it, and went in.[1] She found herself in a room where was a woman weaving.

"What are you doing?" she asked.

"I am weaving swaddling clothes for the king's son, who is about to be born."

Then she went into another room and found a woman sewing.

"What are you doing?" she asked.

"I am making robes for the king's son, who is about to be born."

In the next room she found a shoemaker.

"What are you doing?" she asked again.

"Making shoes for the king's son, who is about to be born."

Then she went back, locked the box again, and held the candle low down to look at her husband. As she did so a drop of wax fell on his neck, and he woke.

"You have betrayed me," said he, "and must lose me."

In an instant she found herself standing above-ground, her *zappa* over her shoulder, and clad only in her nightdress, poor thing. She went a little way, and found the king's washerwomen at work. They gave her some clothes and said:—

"You see that hill yonder? Walk all day till you come to it, and there you will find a shepherd, who will take you in for to-night." (But really, they had been sent by her husband, and so had the shepherd.)

The poor girl walked all day, and in the evening came to the shepherd. He received her kindly, gave her supper and a bed, and in the morning made her some coffee and gave her breakfast. Then he said:—

"You see that other hill, over there? Walk all day till you come to it, there you will find my brother" (but really it was himself) "who will be kind to you. And now take this chestnut, but be sure you don't open it unless you are in great need."

So the poor thing walked all day until she reached the second hill and found the second shepherd. He gave her supper, a bed, and coffee in the morning, and then said:—

"Go on to the next hill, where you will find a third shepherd, my brother; ask him to take you in. Now take this nut, but be sure you don't crack it unless you are in great need."

That evening she reached the third shepherd, who treated her as the others had done. In the morning he said to her:—

"You must pass this first hill, and then you will find another; go up that, and you will come to a palace. In the palace lives a queen, who lost her little son, and who now receives poor women, and has them taken care of for forty days; she will be kind to you." Then he gave her a walnut, saying:—"Mind you don't crack it, unless you are in great need."

So the poor creature walked and walked and walked, and in the evening reached the palace.

The queen received her kindly, and had her taken care of for forty days. Then she sent a servant, who said:—

"The queen says you must be off, she can't keep you any longer."

"Oh dear, oh dear," said the poor woman, "whatever shall I do? I have nowhere to go. I'll crack the chestnut."

She did so, and out jumped a lovely little golden dog, which capered about and caressed her and fawned on her. She sent it as a present to the queen, who said:—

"Why, this woman is richer than I am; let her stay forty days more."

So the poor thing remained forty days longer, and then the servant came again to send her away. This time she cracked the nut, and out came two beautiful golden capons. These, too, she sent to the queen, who said:—

"This is certainly a wonderful woman, let her stay another forty days."

At the end of the forty days the queen sent the servant again, saying:—

"You'll eat up all my kingdom. Be off with you."

Then the woman cracked the walnut, and found a beautiful golden wool-winder, which she sent to the queen.

"I never had such things," said the queen, "this woman is richer than I am. Let her stop as long as she likes."

Then the poor woman was glad indeed, and stayed there quietly until she gave birth to a little daughter. The servant took the baby into the kitchen to put on the swaddling-bands; while she was doing so a beautiful white dove alighted on the window-sill, and said:—

> "If the cocks no longer sang,
> If the bells no longer rang,
> If you knew this, oh mother mine,
> Lovely you'd be, oh daughter mine."

Then the servant went to the queen and told her what had happened.

"To-morrow I'll come myself," said she, "and see the dove, and hear what it says."

As soon as she had heard it, she had all the cocks in the town killed, and all the bells tied up: and the next morning she carried the babe into the kitchen herself. No sooner had she sat down than the dove alighted on her shoulder. She unswaddled the baby, and the little thing stretched out its tiny arms in joy at feeling itself free. As it did so, it touched the dove, who was instantly changed into a handsome young man. The queen knew him for her son, the poor woman for her husband, and there was great feasting and joy in all the palace. If they're not alive, they must be dead: if they're not dead, they're still living.

TERESINA, LUISA, AND THE BEAR

CLEMENTINA had been doing her shopping in the village and now the two children and I were walking home with her. It was near the time of sunset, and the Apennines, blue-purple as the sun gradually dropped behind them, unrolled themselves before us, chain behind chain, as we advanced along the road with the valley on the left and the chestnut-covered hill on the right.

"A story, *nonna mia*," begged I, and "A story," echoed the children: "tell us the story about Teresina." So Clementina began:—

Once there was a woman who had two daughters: at least, one was a daughter, and the other a step-daughter. Now the daughter, named Luisa, was ugly and wicked: but the step-daughter, Teresina, was so good and beautiful that everybody loved her. This made Luisa very jealous, and she began to think what she might do to get rid of Teresina. One evening she said to her mother:—

"Mother, send Teresina into the woodhouse to-night, so that the bear may come and eat her while she's alone in the forest."

So the mother gave Teresina a piece of dry bread and said to her:—

"Take your distaff and go and spin wool in the woodhouse to-night."

"Very well," said Teresina, and went out into the forest; and the dog and the cat went with her.

When she got into the woodhouse she shut the door, pulled out her piece of bread, and began to eat her supper.

"Miaou, miaou," said pussy, and patted her arm.

"Ah, poor little pussy, are you hungry too? Here's a piece of bread for you."

"Bow-wow," said the dog, and put his front paws on her knee.

"Yes, little one, here's a piece for you too, you must be hungry, I'm sure."

When she had finished her bread she began to spin, but she had not been at work long when she heard a knock at the door.

"Who's there?"

"The bear," was the answer.

"Oh dear, what shall I do?" said Teresina.

"Tell him you'll let him in when he brings you a dress like the sun," said the dog.

So Teresina did as she was advised; and the bear went in a very short time to Paris, and came back with a dress as beautiful as the sun.

"Tell him he must bring one like the moon," said the cat.

The bear brought that too.

"Now ask for one like the sky with the stars in it," said the dog: and the bear soon came back with that as well.

"What shall I do now?" asked Teresina.

"You must ask for a nice silk handkerchief for your head."

So the bear brought the most beautiful that ever was seen.

"What can I say next?" said Teresina, "I shall have to let him in."

"No, no, ask for a fan."

The bear brought a fan such as Teresina had never imagined.

"One thing more," said the dog; "ask for a chest of linen."

Again Teresina followed the animal's advice, and almost immediately the bear appeared at the door with the chest of linen. But just as he arrived the sun rose, and he was obliged to go away. Then Teresina put the chest on her head, took up her dresses, her handkerchief and her fan, and went away home with the cat and the dog.

When she appeared among the trees before the house, Luisa was first of all very much disappointed, for she thought that the bear had certainly eaten her sister; but when Teresina showed all her beautiful things, then Luisa fairly cried with spite.

"Give them to me, Teresina," she said; "you must and shall give them to me!"

"No, no," said Teresina, "they're mine and I shall keep them."

"Then, mother," exclaimed Luisa, "let me go to the woodhouse to-night. I will go to the woodhouse to-night and see the bear. I will, I will!"

So the mother gave her a nice slice of polenta with plenty of cheese, and in the evening Luisa went off, followed by the cat and dog.

"Miaou, miaou," said the cat, when Luisa began to eat.

"Bow-wow," said the dog.

"Get away, ugly beasts," said Luisa, and kicked at them with her heavy nailed boots. Then came a knock at the door.

"What shall I do?" asked Luisa.

"Open," said the cat and the dog, "it's the bear with the dresses."

So Luisa opened the door, and the bear came and ate her all up.

But Teresina put on her beautiful dresses when she went out walking: and one day the king's son saw her, and loved her because she looked so good and beautiful. So Teresina married the prince, and afterwards became queen of the land.

"Are there any bears about the mountains now, nonna?" I asked, when the story was finished.

"No, there are none now. I saw one once, though. A man was leading it about with a chain."

"I saw one once, too," said little Elisa. "It was at a fair at that village over there," pointing to a cluster of houses on the hillside.

"And what was it like?" I asked.

"It was covered with hair, had two legs, the head of a horse and the feet of a Christian."

And the child really believed she was describing what she had seen.

A TUSCAN BLUEBEARD

Soon after this we reached Clementina's house. The old woman gave the beef-steak and the medicine to her neighbour (whose husband, just returned from Maremma, was down with fever), took up a large wicker-covered flask, and called us to go with her to the "*fonte fresca*" to get water. So we moved off through the chestnut woods, and soon found the spring, half-hidden by the ferns and long grass. It fully deserved its name and reputation; the water was so cold and sparkling as to be almost exhilarating, and I felt a sudden new sympathy with the feeling which prompted the Greeks to such efforts to obtain the water of well-known springs.

When we had emerged from the wood on our way back, Clementina put down her flask and seated herself on a bank with her back to the sunset. We threw ourselves on the grass at her feet, and the old woman, beginning again, told us the following version of our old friend Bluebeard:—

Once upon a time there was a woman who had three daughters. One day a sexton knocked at her door and said:—

"Good wife, give me a piece of bread."

The woman said to the eldest daughter:—

"Take the poor man a piece of bread: he looks very wretched."

But when the girl got outside the door with the bread, the sexton said:—

"It's you I want," and he caught her up and carried her away.

After a while they reached a field where there was a hole in the ground. In the hole the girl saw steps, and when they got to the bottom of these, she found herself in the most beautiful palace she had ever seen.

"Now," said the man, "this palace shall belong to you. I shall be away all day, but shall come back every evening; so you need not be lonely. While I am away you may amuse yourself as you like. Here are the keys; you can explore the whole palace except the room which this key opens; there you are never to go."

"Very well," said the girl, "I won't."

"Take this ring," continued the man, putting one on her finger. "So long as the gold remains bright, I shall know you have been obedient. When it is cloudy, I shall know you have opened the door."

For some days the girl was quite happy exploring the wonders of this underground palace; but little by little she began to want to see what was in the room which was forbidden her; and at last the desire to open that door quite overcame her dread of punishment. She put in the key, turned it, pushed open the door, and went in.

She found herself in a marble courtyard opening on to a beautiful garden. In the middle of the courtyard was a pond, in which was swimming a lovely gold-red fish.

"Oh, I must catch you," said the girl, and plunged her hand into the water. But the fish bit her so sharply that she withdrew her hand immediately, and then she saw that the ring was covered with blood. She rubbed and rubbed, but the blood would not come off; the ring was stained and cloudy, and sadly she went out, locking the door behind her.

When the man came home that night he found her sad and dejected.

"Ah," said he, "you have disobeyed me. Let me see the ring."

She tried to hide her hand, but it was no good. He looked at the ring, and then cut off her head, and put head and body against one of the columns in the marble courtyard.

After that he went back to the girl's home, and again asked for bread.

"Go," said the mother to the second daughter, "carry the poor man something to eat."

But when the second daughter came to him he treated her as he had done the first. He carried her off to the underground palace, gave her the keys, and a ring, and told her, too, that she might do anything she liked, except open that door.

It happened to the second as it had done to the first. She got tired of wandering about the palace with nothing to do, opened the door, and went into the marble courtyard. She, too, tried to catch the fish; she, too, was bitten; her ring became cloudy, and she was beheaded and put beside her sister.

Then the man returned, and carried away the youngest girl. Now the youngest is always cleverer than her elder sisters; and so it happened in this case. After she had spent some time in the palace, she, too, determined to open the forbidden door. So she took off her ring, put it in her work-basket, and went in. She tried to catch the fish, as her sisters had done, and then began to wander about. She soon saw her sisters' heads and bodies, and that made her sad. When it was near evening she left the courtyard, put on her ring, and went to meet her husband as brightly and cheerfully as ever.

"Ah," said the man, "I can see that you have not disobeyed me. You're a dear, good little wife."

Every day, as soon as her husband was gone, the girl took her work into the garden and sat there, knitting or playing with the fish, but she was unhappy because of her sisters.

One morning as she was at work she saw a little lizard without a tail; the tail was lying on the ground beside it. She watched the creature and saw it bite a leaf off a certain plant, turn its head over its back, and touch its body and its tail with the leaf. Instantly tail and body grew together, and the lizard ran off quite merrily.

"Aha," thought the girl, "now I know what to do!" So she picked the plant, went into the courtyard, put her sisters' heads on to their respective bodies, touched the necks with the plants, and there were her sisters quite well again. Then she took them upstairs and hid them.

That evening she said to her husband, "I am afraid my mother must be very unhappy. She is old and poor, and now there is no one to work for her or take care of her. Let me go and see her."

"No," said the man; "I can't spare you."

"Well, then, let me fill a chest with clothes and money, and you shall carry it to her."

"Very well," said the man; "have it ready by to-morrow morning."

So the girl put linen and gold into a chest. Then she made her eldest sister get in, and shut down the lid.

"Now," she said to her husband, "you must not set down the chest at all: remember, I can see you all the way. Go straight there and back again, for I want you at home."

The man put the chest on his head and set off. After a time he began to want to put down his burden for a little, and said to himself:—

"My wife can't possibly see me; there's this hill between me and her": and he began to set down the chest.

"Do you think I can't see you?" a voice said. "Silly man, I can see you everywhere."

"Oh dear, oh dear," said the man to himself, "what a clever wife mine is! She can see me even through a hill. And how fond of me she is! She knows what I am doing wherever I am." So he staggered on to his mother-in-law's, threw down the box, and went home again.

A little while after the second sister was sent home in the same way, and now the girl began to think how she could get away herself. One evening she said to her husband:—

"I want you to take some more things to my mother. I shall get everything ready to-night. Don't wake me in the morning before you go, as I shall come to bed very late. I have to make the bread."

The man went off to bed, and the girl set to work. She made a great doll of dough and put it in her bed; then she put clothes and money into the chest, crept in herself, and pulled down the lid.

The next morning the man got up early. "Wife, wife," he shouted, "good-bye!"

No answer. "Ah, I forgot, she was up late making bread. She's a dear little wife, and works very hard."

So he crept on tiptoe to her bedside, saw the figure under the clothes, and went out as quietly as he had gone in.

Then he took the chest and started. Again he wanted to set down his burden, again the warning voice stopped him, and at last he flung down the box at his mother-in-law's door, declaring that this was the last he would bring her.

When he got home he called, "Wife! wife!"

Still no answer. "What, is she still asleep? She must be tired"; and he went to shake her. Then he found that there was no wife there, but only a figure of dough, and that he was alone once more in his underground palace.

TASSA

CLEMENTINA had enticed me to her cottage with the promise of country beans cooked in country fashion, to be followed by a story under the chestnut woods. So at about four in the afternoon, when the heat of the day was over in the breezy mountain village, I sauntered through the street, past the swarming black-eyed children, and the cheerful, smiling washerwomen busy at the tank under the pump, out on the white road beyond; and, gazing now at the landscape on the left, now at the ever-varying forms of the Apennines before me—

> "Ever some new head or breast of them,
> Thrusts into view,"

says Browning—now climbing the bank on the right for flowers or mountain-strawberries, I arrived, after half an hour's stroll, at the little hamlet of Ciecafumo.

There stood the cluster of smoke-blackened cottages, with the large patch of rye, beans, etc. (apparently common property), before them, against a background of magnificent chestnut trees. Passing under a picturesque archway, and crossing a cobbled space which did duty as a street, I pushed open the wooden door of Clementina's house. Before me was a flight of stairs which might have been washed towards the end of the last century: on the right the kitchen; and, dim in the blue, arching wood-smoke, Clementina, with eyes as bright as ever under her kerchief; and sprightly little Nella, barefooted, and, still more extraordinary, bareheaded.

It was a large, low room, with stone walls and a gaping plank ceiling, which formed also the floor of the room above, all encrusted with the black lichen-like deposit, harder than the stone itself, produced by the smoke of wood-fires. In one corner was a tiny window, and on the same side with it the hearth, with a wooden roof over it in lieu of chimney. The wood-fire, the cat, the red pipkin with the old woman bending over it, formed a pretty interior against the dark shadows of the great stack of brushwood which, with a flight of very rickety stairs, occupied the further end of the room.

"Where do the stairs lead, Nonna?" I asked.

"Oh, those lead into the cat's rooms. You can go up if you like, but I advise you not to. It's years since I have been there, and I expect they're rather dirty."

It need hardly be said that I did *not* go up. The beans being now ready, a space was cleared on one of the two tables, which, loaded with most heterogeneous material, were propped up against the wall opposite the fire. Above the tables was the one patch of colour on the black walls—a coloured print or so of saints, a couple of rosaries, and a tiny hanging tin lamp. The old woman spread a coarse, newly-washed table-napkin on the space she had cleared, and placed on it a hunch of bread (brought that morning from the village), one glass, a little bottle of oil, and some salt in a piece of paper. The wicker-covered water-flask was put on the ground beside us; three chairs were produced, and three soup-plates, with brass spoons. Then the beans were divided and dressed with oil and salt, the bread was carved into three parts with a great clasp-knife from the old woman's pocket, and we made a very excellent and nourishing meal. The one glass did duty for all three of us, being rinsed out with a peculiar jerk on to the stone floor after each had drunk.

"Now the story, Nonna," said I.

So Clementina took up her knitting, and, locking the door behind us, we went out into the fresh, sweet evening air. We sat down under a huge chestnut tree. A number of little girls came clustering around us, busily engaged in making chestnut-leaf pockets for their wild strawberries and whortle-berries, and the old woman began:—

Once upon a time there was a poor woman who had one daughter. One day, as this daughter was out in the forest getting firewood she struck her axe into a hollow tree. As soon as she had done so, a beautiful lady appeared and said to her:—

"Will you come with me, little girl? I will take care of you, and give you everything you want."

So the little girl said yes, she would go, and the lady, who was really a fairy, took her to a beautiful palace.

"Now," said this fairy, "when you're alone, and want me, you must call me Tassa, but when anyone else is with you, you must call me Aunt. You won't always see me, but as soon as you call me I shall come to you. You may do what you like and go where you like in this palace."

So the girl lived for some time in the palace in the forest, and grew more and more beautiful every day. At last it happened that the king's son, out hunting in that forest, came to the palace and saw the girl at the window. He rode round trying to find a door, but there was none.

"Let me come in and talk to you," he said to the girl. So she went into the

26

next room, and called out "Tassa."

"What do you want, pretty maiden?"

"The king's son asks to come and talk to me."

"Let him come."

And immediately the prince saw a door and went in. After a little while he said:—

"I should like to marry you; you are the most beautiful woman I have seen."

So the girl went into the next room and called "Tassa."

"What is it, pretty maiden?"

"The prince wants to marry me."

"Let him come in a week with all his court and fetch you."

Then the prince went away, and the fairy gave the girl a box, saying:—

"If you want to remain beautiful, take this box with you; and don't forget to say good-bye to me before you go."

At the end of the week the prince came with a great train of carriages and courtiers to fetch his bride, and the girl was so dazzled by the splendour, and excited at the thought of marrying the prince, that she forgot to say good-bye to the fairy, and forgot her box till she was in the carriage. Then she suddenly remembered it, jumped out, and ran upstairs to the cupboard where she had put it. Now this was a cupboard in the wall, and the door pushed up as a shutter might do. The girl raised the door and put her head in to look for the box, when bang! down came the shutter on her neck.

"Tassa, Tassa," she shouted.

"What do you want, ugly wench?"

"I forgot to say good-bye to you. And oh, please let me out."

Then the cupboard door was raised, and the girl went downstairs. But when she appeared everyone began to laugh, for she had a sheep's head!

The prince made her get into the carriage, and then pulled down all the blinds, so that no one might see his ugly bride; and when he got home he had her put into the sheep stable.

Now there were three beautiful women at the king's palace who all wanted to marry the prince, and the prince did not know which to choose. So he brought some wool and said:—

"The one who spins this best shall be my wife"; and he gave some wool to the girl with the sheep's head as well.

The three women set to work immediately and span and span with all their might; but the poor girl in the stable threw hers into the gutter and sat down to cry, while the others came and mocked her. At last it was the eve of the day on which they were to go before the prince, and the girl sobbed and sobbed, and began to call out "Tassa, Tassa!"

"What do you want, ugly wench?"

"I've thrown my wool away, and I don't know what to do."

"Take this filbert, and when you come before the prince crack it. But you don't deserve to be helped."

The next day the whole court was assembled and the three women gave their skeins of wool, and then the prince turned to the girl and said:—

"What have you done?"

"Baa, baa," said she, and cracked the filbert. There was a skein of the finest wool that could be imagined, and all said that the sheep had done best.

Then the prince gave each one a puppy, and said:—

"The one whose puppy grows into the most beautiful dog shall be my bride."

So the three women took their puppies, and brushed them and combed them and washed them and fed them, till they were so fat they could hardly move; but the poor girl let hers run away.

The women came and mocked her as before, but all she could say was "Baa, baa!"

Again it was the eve of the day when they were to appear before the prince, and again the girl sat sobbing in her stable and calling "Tassa, Tassa!"

"What do you want, ugly wench?"

"My dog has run away, and to-morrow we go before the king."

"Take this walnut, and crack it as you did the filbert. But you don't deserve to be helped."

The next day the whole court was assembled again. The three women presented their dogs, which waddled about and behaved very dirtily and badly.

"And what have you done?" said the prince to the girl.

"Baa, baa," said she, and cracked the walnut. Out jumped the most lovely tiny dog, with a golden collar and golden tinkling bells; he fawned upon the king and the prince, and quite won their hearts by his pretty manners.

"One more trial," said the prince. "All appear before me again in a week's time, and I will marry the most beautiful."

All that week the three women washed themselves, and scented themselves, and rubbed themselves till they rubbed the skin off, and pomaded their hair till it shone like a looking-glass; but the girl sat among the sheep and wept.

On the last day of the week the women began to put on their fine dresses and ornaments; and the unhappy girl sobbed more bitterly than ever, and called out, "Tassa, Tassa!"

"What do you want, pretty maiden?"

"To-morrow we go before the prince. What shall I do?"

"Go with the others: and if he marries you don't forget to say good-bye to me."

The next morning the three women with their grand dresses, and their pomade, and their scent, strutted boldly in before the court and the prince.

"Go to the stable and bring the fourth," commanded the prince: and one of the courtiers went down.

Soon the door opened and the room was filled with a blaze of light, as the beautiful maiden, sheep no longer, entered and knelt humbly before the king.

"That is my bride," said the prince, as he raised her and kissed her: "You others may go."

So a grand wedding-feast was prepared, and this time the girl did not forget to say good-bye to the fairy who had been so kind to her.

PADRE ULIVO

"Strange, lingering echoes of the old demon-worship might perhaps be even now caught by the diligent listener among the grey-haired peasantry," says George Eliot, speaking of the Midland Counties of England. Stranger yet, perhaps, is the survival of the old pagan spirit, the haunting echo of old pagan legend, which any visitor to the hills of Tuscany may verify. Let him join the peasants as they meet now in one house, now in another, to spend the long winter evenings round the fire; or let him stroll, in the early autumn, into some low, dark kitchen where neighbours sit among piles of chestnut twigs, busily stripping off the leaves and making them into bundles for winter use in the baking of chestnut cakes (*necci*). There, among *stornelli* and *rispetti*, he may well chance upon some such shrewd, quaint tale as the following:—

Once upon a time there was a man called Padre Ulivo. He was always cheerful, always singing, and very fond of good company. He had a barrel of wine in the cellar, and every evening his friends used to come and see him, sit round the fire, eat, drink, sing, and lead a merry life. But at last the barrel was empty, and all his provisions run out, so that he had nothing more to offer to those who came, and all his pleasant evenings were at an end. Now everyone avoided him, and his cottage grew dull and lonely. One night he had just enough flour left for one small cake.

"Well," said he, "I'll make a little *schiacciata* this evening, bake it in the ashes, and to-morrow I must take what God sends."

So he made the *schiacciata*, ate half of it, and got into bed. He had not been there long before he heard a knock at the door.

"Who's there?" he called out.

"Padre Ulivo," said a voice from outside, "we want to come in and warm ourselves at your fire; open the door to us."

So Padre Ulivo jumped out of bed, opened the door, and there were twelve men outside.

"Wait a minute while I put on my trousers," said he, for he was in his shirt.

"Now, Padre Ulivo," said one of the men, "we want something to eat."

"Something to eat! How can I give you that when I have nothing in the house! I made a little *schiacciata* of my last flour this evening. Look, here's the bit I've not eaten."

"No, no; you must give us something to eat—we're hungry."

"But, indeed, I don't do it to deceive you. I have nothing; absolutely nothing."

"Go and look again in the cupboard."

"But what's the good? It's empty. Do you believe that I want to deceive you?"

"Go and look, at all events."

So Padre Ulivo opened the cupboard, and found it quite full of meat and bread, and everything nice. Quite full! and of such good things as he had never hoped to have.

"Oh!" said he, "don't think I was deceiving you; there really was nothing there last time I went to it."

So he laid the table and they began to eat.

"But we want wine," said the man; "go to the cellar and get some."

"I have none," said Padre Ulivo; "I used up all mine some time ago."

"Go and see."

"But it's no good; my barrel is quite empty. Indeed it is not because I am greedy. I have none left."

"Go and see. We'll come too."

So they all went down to the cellar.

"You see," said Padre Ulivo, tapping the barrel. "Listen how hollow it sounds!"

"Draw out the spigot."

He did so, and immediately there spurted out such a stream of wine as knocked him right against the opposite wall.

"Oh, oh!" said he. "I swear it was empty last time I came here."

Then he filled a big jug, and they all went upstairs and made a good supper.

"Now we want to sleep here," said the men.

"But I have only one bed," answered Padre Ulivo; "and there are thirteen of us! I know what I'll do, though; I'll put the mattress on the floor, and we must manage the best way we can."

So he put the mattress on the floor, spread sheets on it, and they slept comfortably, some on the mattress and some on the bed.

The next morning the men went away, and Padre Ulivo accompanied them for some little distance on their journey, walking behind with one who was especially friendly.

"The one in front," said this man, "the most important of us all, is Dominiddio[2] himself. Go and ask him a favour."

So Padre Ulivo ran on, and threw himself on his knees in the road.

"What do you want?" said Dominiddio. "I will grant you whatever you ask for."

"I want that anyone who sits down on my chair may be unable to rise without my permission."

"Be it so."

And Padre Ulivo returned to his companion.

"Have you asked a favour?"

"Yes, and it's granted."

"What did you ask?"

Padre Ulivo told him.

"Oh, you stupid man! But go and ask another favour quickly. And mind it's something great, and something really for yourself. Remember you are speaking to Dominiddio."

Padre Ulivo ran on again and knelt down.

"What do you want this time? You shall have it."

"Let anyone who gets up into my fig-tree be unable to come down without my permission."

"Very well; it shall be so."

And Padre Ulivo came back leaping for joy.

"Well, and what did you ask for?"

Padre Ulivo told him.

"Oh, you fool! Go again, you will get one more favour; but mind you ask for something really good for yourself."

He wanted him to ask to go to Paradise.

"Again!" said Dominiddio, when he saw Padre Ulivo in the dust before him. "Well, this is the last time. What do you want?"

"Let me always win at cards, no matter whom I may be playing with."

"Be it so. And now no more."

Padre Ulivo came back to his companion singing for joy.

"What have you asked for this time? Something really great?"

"Oh, yes," said Padre Ulivo, and told him.

"Well, you've lost your chance now. Good-bye."

With that he left him and Padre Ulivo went home.

Now his jolly times began again. His barrel of wine never ran dry, and his cupboard never grew empty. Everybody came to see him. They ate, drank, and led a merry life.

*　　*　　*　　*　　*

But Padre Ulivo grew old; and one day Death came to him.

"Oh, how do you do?" said Padre Ulivo. "You want me, do you? Well, I was just beginning to fear you had forgotten me, and to wonder where you could be. Sit down and take a rest, and then I'll come with you."

So Death sat down on the chair in the chimney-corner, while Padre Ulivo piled on wood and made a splendid blaze.

"Now we must go," said Death, when he was warm. "Oh, oh! what's this?" For when he tried to get up the chair stuck to him and he could not move. "Oh, oh!" And he pulled at the chair that seemed glued firmly to him. "Padre Ulivo, let me go! I have to go for the carpenter's daughter before sundown. Oh, oh! I can't get up. You've bewitched me."

"Promise not to come back for a hundred years, and you shall go free."

"A hundred! A hundred and one, if you like! Only take the spell off."

So Padre Ulivo gave him permission to rise, and Death went away.

*　　*　　*　　*　　*

Things went on as usual for the hundred years, with feasting and merry-making. But at last, as Padre Ulivo was among his friends, Death appeared again.

"Yes, yes, I'm ready. But let us have a feast of figs first. See what splendid fruit there! I and my friends had as much as we wanted yesterday, it's your turn to-day. Go up and help yourself; I am too old to climb."

So Death went up the tree and picked and ate to his heart's content.

"Now we must go," said he. "Hullo! I can't get down. Oh, Padre Ulivo, you've bewitched me again!" And he stretched out now an arm, now a leg, and twisted and turned; but it was all of no good, and the others stood below laughing at him.

"Oh, Padre Ulivo! I'll leave you another hundred years, if you'll only let me get down."

"Very well; then you may come."

So Death climbed down and went away.

✳   ✳   ✳   ✳   ✳

When the hundred years were passed, he came and stood outside the cottage.

"Padre Ulivo, Padre Ulivo, come out! I shan't come near your house this time. I don't want to be tricked again."

"Oh, no, I'm coming. Wait till I get my jacket."

So he put on his coat and went with Death.

On the way they met the Devil.

"Ah, good morning, Padre Ulivo" (one can see they knew each other very well), "so you're coming my way, are you?"

"To be sure I am. But let's have a game at cards first."

"By all means! What shall we play for?"

"For souls. A soul for every game."

"Good! I'm not afraid. Nobody ever beat the Devil yet at cards."

So they began, and Padre Ulivo won game after game.

The Devil got very angry and spit flames of fire from sheer rage, as he saw the crowd of souls collecting round Padre Ulivo.

"This will never do," he said at last. "I shall have no fire left to warm myself at if I go on losing my fuel at this rate. Padre Ulivo, take your souls and be off. I have had enough of you."

They left the Devil boiling over with fury, and went and knocked at the gate of Heaven.

"Who's there?"

"Padre Ulivo."

"I'll go and ask if you may come in." Then, after a little time: "Dominiddio says you may come in, if you're alone; but you must not bring anyone else."

"Go and tell Dominiddio that when he came to me I let him in with all his friends. He ought to do the same by me."

The porter took the message, and then came and opened the gates.

"Dominiddio says you may all come in together."

So they threw themselves down in the armchairs of Paradise, and enjoyed themselves for ever.

Surely a tale of this kind is an eloquent commentary on the mind of the people who have preserved it. The shrewd cunning, the frank materialism, the lavish generosity, so long as there is anything to be generous with ("since it's there," they will say as they offer or use the last of their store), are all strongly marked features among these peasants.

At the same time, the story itself suggests a curious feeling that we have to do with Jupiter and Mercury transformed in the crucible of Christian history and Catholic dogma. The transformation is an instructive one in many ways, and it would be interesting to know whether it has taken place in any other country besides Italy.

THE SOUND AND SONG OF THE LOVELY SIBYL

It was old 'Drea I was talking to, this time. Andrea was my peasant friend's father, a small, infirm-looking man, about eighty years of age, of great shrewdness and penetration. We were sitting in the little kitchen garden beside the bean-vines, and as we chatted his eye roamed continually over the valley and the hills beyond, with the expression of one accustomed to render an account to himself of all he saw. He told me of his life as foreman to the great landowner of that part of the country; of his journeyings from one outlying farm to another, to collect the half of the farm-produce which is the due of the owner of the soil; of his experiences as head forester down in Maremma; of the power of the priests in his young days, the days of the Archduke Peter Leopold. "Why in those days," said he, "two lines from the parish priest would send a man to the galleys for eight years without trial. There were Giovanni and Sandro, lived opposite the post office, in that house with a railing—you know it?—well, they're old men now; but they have each served their eight years as convicts, nobody ever knew why."

At last he asked me if I should like a story. 'Drea was a well-known story-teller and improviser, so I said nothing would please me better, and he began[3]:—

Once upon a time there was a knight who had three beautiful daughters. Now this knight determined to go to the Holy Land to fight for the tomb of our Lord, but he did not know what to do with his three daughters. At length a friend said:—"Build a tower for them," and the idea was such a good one that he adopted it. He had a tall tower built, with three bedrooms and a sitting-room at the top of it; he locked the door at the foot and provided his daughters with a basket and a long rope with which to draw up their food. Then he gave each girl a diamond ring, and said:—

"So long as you are good, the diamonds will be bright and victorious, but if you do wrong I shall find them dull on my return."

So he went away to fight the Saracens.

A little while after he had gone, the eldest daughter going to draw up the basket one morning, saw a poor man down below shivering with cold.

"Oh, sisters," she said, "look at that poor man: shall we draw him up and

37

feed him and warm him?"

"Do as you like," said they; "we won't be answerable for the results."

So the girl bade the man get into the basket, drew him up, made a blazing fire, warmed him thoroughly, and gave him some dinner.

"Now you must go," she said after a time, "you are warm, you have been fed, you have rested; what more do you want?"

"I must have supper with you." To that the girl agreed, and then again told him to go away.

"I must sleep with you to-night," said he.

Well, the girl did not know what to do, so she submitted.

The next morning after breakfast, the second daughter said to the man:—

"Now be off, we've had enough of you."

"No, I am going to stay to dinner": and after dinner it was:—"No, I am going to stay to supper," and after supper the same thing as before.

The next day it was the third sister's turn. Now the younger sisters are always more cunning than the elder ones, and this was no exception to the rule.

As before, the man stopped to breakfast, dinner and supper; but after supper the girl went to her room, saying to him:—"Wait till I call you."

Now the tower had been built in a hurry and the floors were of plank only, not of brick or stone. Of this the maiden took advantage. She raised three or four planks just inside the door and then called:—"My light's out, come and light it."

The man ran to do so, but fell down the hole to the bottom of the tower; and as it was a high one he was killed by the fall.

The next morning the three sisters looked at their rings, but only that of the youngest was bright, the others were dull and clouded.

"What shall we do?" said the girls.

"I'll tell you," said the youngest; "we'll sit all in a row, and pass my ring from one to another so cleverly that nobody shall notice."

Presently their father came back. They did as their sister advised, and he was quite satisfied. Then they all went home to live in their old house and had a merry time of it.

One day, as the eldest was looking out of the window she saw the king's baker.

"Ah, what a handsome man," said she. "If he were to marry me I would make, in one day, enough bread to last the court for a year."

These words were repeated to the baker; he married her and she managed to keep her promise.

A little while afterwards the second daughter was looking out of window when she spied the king's pastry-cook.

"How I should like to marry that fine-looking man," said she. "I would make enough cakes in a day to last a year."

As before, the words were repeated; the girl had her wish, and managed to keep her promise.

But the third daughter saw the king's son, and said, "If the king's son were to marry me I would bring him three children, two boys and a girl, each with the red cross of a knight on his chest."

This saying was repeated to the prince who married the girl and almost immediately afterwards became king. But he had not been king long before a terrible war broke out, and he had to leave his bride and go far away to fight. He put her under the charge of his mother, with strict injunctions that he should receive information as to whether his wife had kept her promise or not. Now the queen-mother was a wicked woman, who hated her daughter-in-law because she was not a princess by birth, but only the daughter of a poor knight; and the two elder sisters also hated the queen, being jealous of her, because they had to bow before her and do her homage. So these three women consulted together, and sent for a wicked witch to help them injure the poor queen. The queen had three children as she had promised, two boys and a girl, each with the red cross of a knight on his chest; but as soon as they were born, the witch let three black puppies run about the room, and took away the children and put them on the river-bank in the forest hard by. Then she sent word to the king:—

"Your wife has brought you three black dogs."

"Let her and them be well taken care of," wrote he. But the witch and the queen-mother changed the letter into:—

"Let her be walled in at the foot of the stairs, and let everyone who goes by spit on her"; and this was done. Now we will go back to the children.

In the forest there lived a hermit; he heard small voices crying, went and looked, and found the little ones. He took them to his hut, and tended them, and they grew up like flowers, fine and strong, with the red cross always in front.

After a time the king returned from the wars; and, when he reached his palace, saw his wife at the foot of the stairs and heard all that had been done to her. At first he was angry, but they persuaded him that it was all as it should be, and he left his queen there, thin and ill. Still he was very unhappy, and to console himself he went out hunting. In the forest there lived a fairy, a friend of the hermit's. She it was who had led the hermit to the children, and now she guided the king to the hermit's hut. There were the children, beautiful as flowers, each with the red cross.

"That reminds me of what my wife once said," said he. "All come and have dinner with me to-morrow."

With that he went home and told what had happened. So the queen-mother called the witch, and said:—

"What shall we do? We shall be found out."

"No, no," said the witch; "you leave all to me; it will be all right."

Meanwhile the hermit had gone to ask advice from the fairy.

"You must all go," said she. "When you come to the palace you will see a beautiful pale woman walled in at the foot of the stairs, and you will be told to spit on her; but you must refuse to do it. That is the children's mother."

The three children and the hermit went to the palace.

"Spit on that woman," commanded the guard.

"No," said they all; "such a thing would be very improper."

"Then you can't go in," said the soldier. And so loud a dispute arose that the king came himself; and when he heard what was the matter, he brought them in gladly, and made them sit down at table. Then the witch who was there told a wicked lie.

"These children," said she, "have said that they can bring the Sound and Song of the Lovely Sibyl." But they had not promised anything of the kind.

"Very well," said the king, "let them come back with it here."

So the hermit and the children went away, and the eldest boy set out.

"If I am not back in seven days," said he, "you may know that something has happened to me."

He rode on till he came to a hermit with a white beard sitting by the roadside.

"Where are you going?" asked this hermit.

"Well-bred people don't put questions of that sort," answered the prince and passed on.

After the seven days were gone the second brother determined to try his luck, as the first had not yet returned. He, too, met the hermit, received the same question, gave the same answer, and rode away.

Now another seven days had elapsed, and the sister resolved to set out; but first she asked the advice of the fairy.

"After some time you will find a white-bearded hermit," said the fairy; "don't answer him as your brothers have done: tell him where you are going, and he will help you."

So when she reached the old man she told him about the quest on which her brothers and herself had set out.

"Just look among my hair," said the hermit, "and comb it. Will you?" And when she had done so he gave her a small rod and a couple of cakes, saying:
—

"Ride on till you come to a palace with two lions in front of it. Throw the cakes to the lions and strike the door with the rod; it will open and in the hall you will see a beautiful girl. She will tell you what you want to know."

So the maiden thanked the hermit and rode off. When she reached the palace she followed the hermit's directions and found the girl.

"Take this rod," said she, "and go into yonder garden. There you will find a bird which will come fluttering round your head and shoulders. Don't attempt to catch it, however, till it reaches your lap; then put both hands over it quickly, hold it tightly, and it will tell you how to free your brothers. That bird is the Sound and Song of the Lovely Sibyl."

The maiden went into the garden and sure enough the bird came fluttering round her as though asking to be caught. But she did not attempt to touch it till it had settled in her lap; then she held it fast with both hands, and the bird said:—

"All these statues you see round you were once men. Those two there are your brothers. Go and touch them with the rod you hold in your hand."

The maiden did as she was bid; her brothers returned to life and they all went away together, carrying the bird with them. When they reached home the fairy said:—

"To-morrow you must go to court. Put the bird in a box and carry it with you; and when the king asks for it, put it on the table, that it may declare the wickedness of the dowager-queen, and the innocence of your mother."

So the next day the three went to the palace and were invited to dine with the king. There were the queen-mother and the witch also present.

"Ah," said the latter sneeringly, "you've kept your promise finely, haven't you?"

"Certainly we have," they answered.

"Why," said the king, "where is the bird?"

They opened the box, and the Sound and Song of the Lovely Sibyl flew on to the table and told the whole black tale of deceit.

Then the queen-mother was burnt in the great public square, and the witch in a smaller square; but the children's mother was crowned queen again amid the shouts of the people, and her husband and her children loved her dearly.

"So," concluded old 'Drea, "innocence triumphs over vice."

THE SNAKE'S BOUDOIR

THIS story was told me by a woman who lives here in Genoa during the winter, but goes up into the mountains for the summer. She says she is quite sure it is true: "*ma poi non lo so.*" I wish I could tell it as well as she did:—

Not far from the villa where she goes in the summer, a stream makes a pool where the women go to do their washing. The pool is surrounded by stones and rocks, and once when the women were washing they noticed a very large snake (*biscia*) gliding among the rocks. They watched him and saw that at a certain place he stopped, put something down behind a stone, and went away. The women went to look, and found his poison like two little horns. In the evening he came back, went to the place where he had hidden his fangs, found them, and fixed them in position again. This happened several days in succession, until one of the women suggested that they should steal the poison-fangs, and see what happened. So the next day they took them into the house with them, and stood at the window to watch the *biscia*. When he came back and could not find his poison fangs, he gave every sign of the utmost surprise; he looked again and again behind the stone where he had left them, as though to say:—"This was certainly the place!" He examined all the stones round the pool, and at last, hissing with rage, began to dash his head against the stones. And the women were watching him all the time from the window. After a while he was so overcome with despair that he gave his head an extra hard knock and split open his skull so that he died.

POMO AND THE GOBLIN HORSE

THIS that I am going to tell you now, the old woman went on, happened when my great grandfather was a little boy. My grandfather used to tell it to my father before he left his native place to marry my mother; for my mother had no brothers, so my father came to live in her country. When my great grandfather was quite young, all the children used to be called in from the streets at sundown, lest they should be frightened by the black horse and his rider who for some time tormented that part of the country. This is the story of the ghost:—

There was in that village a man named Pomo, who was so lazy that he did not like to work; so he said:—

"I'll go for a doctor."

So he went into other districts where no one knew him, and said that he could heal people. But instead he only made them die all the more; and at last he died too. One evening soon after his death, his relations were sitting quietly in their house when they heard a great noise, and looking out, saw all the air full of crows. This went on for several evenings; the house was surrounded by these birds, which flew hither and thither cawing loudly, and then vanished.

At last one evening there were no crows, but they suddenly heard a great clattering of hoofs in the street. They went to the window and looked out and saw a terrible black horse with a man riding on him. The horse came to the doorsteps, put his nose down to the ground, and stood there some time, while the man looked imploringly at the terrified people, but did not speak.

The next evening the horse came again. This time he stood on the threshold, with his nose against the door, but the man did not speak. In the morning the people went to tell the *parroco* and beg him to save them from the devil, for they were sure the black horse could be no other. The *parroco* lived some way off, but he said:—

"If the horse comes to-night, call me at once, and I will see if I can help you."

That night as soon as the hoofs were heard someone ran off to the *parroco*, and the rest huddled into the kitchen so that they might not see the dreadful sight.

But the horse came upstairs, and stood there close by the fire with his nose on the ground and the man hid his face on the horse.

As soon as they heard him coming up the people were so frightened that they jumped out of window, all but one very old woman who feared the fall more than the horse.

Just then the priest came and asked the man, in the name of God, what he wanted. The man answered:—

"I want mass said for me, that I may have rest in the lowest part of hell."

"Well," said the priest, "I will say it to-morrow."

"You must say it at midnight, with your back to the altar," answered the man, "and if you make a single mistake you will have to go to hell along with me."

"I'll do it for you," said the priest, for he was a brave man; and with that the horse and man went away. But when they got among the chestnut trees there was a great noise, and flames of fire; and so the horse and rider vanished. Well, the next day the *parroco* tried to get someone to serve the mass, but he had great difficulty, as everyone was afraid of making a mistake and getting carried off to hell; but at last he persuaded a priest to help him, and towards midnight the two went to the church. The horse and rider stood in the entrance of the west door, and the two priests read mass, with their backs to the altar. They got through without mistake and the devil and the condemned soul disappeared and were never seen again; but the priest who had served the mass was taken up stiff and dumb with terror, and it was many weeks before he could speak again. The *parroco* was less affected; but there was a strange glitter in his eyes for some days; and it was long before he could trust himself to talk of that night.

These stories of demon-steeds are not uncommon in the South. A notable one is that of the terrible "Belludo" of The Alhambra, which Washington Irving uses with such grim effect in his book on the old Moorish pile.

TUSCAN SKETCHES

A TUSCAN COUNTRYSIDE AND THE FESTA AT IL MELO

I HAD left Clementina and the little ones behind me, and had moved further up among the Apennines to a village which, perched on a low hill, overlooks the river and the winding valley. The summits of the mountains all around rise bare and scarped from dark pine and ash woods, while their bases are clothed with chestnuts. Many a long line of soldiers have the villagers seen marching up the valley on the other side of the river which flows at their feet: for the pass is an important one, being the high road from Tuscany into the Modenese. Napoleon III. and Victor Emmanuel rode through it side by side, and old men still relate how the village turned out to salute Emperor and King as they went by. The great Napoleon lives too, in the recollection of the country people, for he drew many soldiers from all the districts round for his "Summer Excursion to Moscow." One cannot vouch, however, for the historical exactitude of some of the stories concerning him. One old woman, for instance, whose husband had saved himself on the ill-fated expedition by cutting open a horse and getting inside it, firmly believed that *le petit Caporal* had perished miserably at Moscow, pickled in a barrel of salt!

Nor are more ancient historical associations wanting. At a very little distance lies the village of Gavinana where the lion-hearted Francesco Ferruccio, trying to burst through the mountains from Pisa to the relief of Florence, was betrayed in 1530 to the Prince of Orange. Captured in the battle which ensued, and carried, covered with wounds which must have been fatal, into the market-place before the Imperialist leader, he was there stabbed to death in cold blood, and expired with the exclamation:—"It is a noble thing to kill a dead man!"

In still more ancient times Catiline passed up the valley when trying to force the Apennines; and the public square bears the name of Piazza Catilina in honour of the monster whom Sallust took so much pains to delineate.

Legends of classical Italian literature, too, still linger here. An inn in the village is called the "Cappel d'Orlando"—(Orlando's Hat)—after Ariosto's famous hero; and a conical-shaped hill on the other side of the valley bears the same name. I asked one of my peasant acquaintances why it was so called, and who Orlando was. The answer was amusing as showing the country conception of the temper and achievements of a knight-errant:—

"Orlando," said the woman, "was a warrior, who rode about looking for someone to fight with. When he came to the top of that hill, he reined in his horse so violently to avoid falling over the precipice that the animal's hoof sank deep into the rock, and the print can still be seen. He took a tremendous leap from the top of the hill down into the village below, but he left his hat behind him. It was afterwards found, and the place was then called Cappel d'Orlando."

Another informant evidently attributed to Orlando the time-annihilating hat for which Carlyle sighs so vainly; for she added to the original story a rider, saying that Orlando, after his marvellous leap, went to Gavinana and was killed fighting against Ferruccio.

Remembrances of an older classical literature than Ariosto abound also. The Muses, Helicon, Troy, are common words among these peasants, whether in speech or in song.

As is mostly the case in Tuscany, the country people are devout; that is to say, they go to mass on Sundays, firmly believe in miracles, and miracle-working images, and are fond of walking in procession. The church of Cutigliano, the village in which I was staying, rejoices in the possession of the entire skeletons of two saints, and of two valuable palladiums—a Madonna which preserves the place from epidemics, and a crucifix which regulates the supply of rain.

On the Feast of the Madonnina, the first of the palladiums is carried in state through the village, the peasants flocking in from all the hamlets near to join in the procession and chant their Ave Marias. The figure is of wood, highly painted, dressed in light blue robes, ornamented with tinsel, and with rings and rosaries on the outstretched hands.

"Did you see my nosegay right in front?" said my landlady that evening. "It was the best there. I love that Madonnina; she saved us from the cholera and from diphtheria. They came right to the foot of the hill, but did not touch us."

"And it was the Madonnina that saved you?" I asked.

"Of course. We took her in procession through the village, and where she passed there was no illness. It's like the uncovering of the crucifix."

"What's that?" I asked.

"Oh, don't you know? There's a crucifix in the church; and when it rains and rains, and the chestnuts are spoiling, we uncover it, and then the rain stops at once."

"Why does it stop when you uncover the crucifix?" I rejoined.

"Oh, Gesú likes it to be uncovered."

"Then why don't you keep it always uncovered?"

"Well, it's not the uncovering, but the candles and prayers and incense that Gesú likes."

"Then Gesú must be vain," remarked the woman's husband, who is something of a heretic, "and the Church says that vanity is a sin."

Each village in the valley has its own special saint, whose feast is the great event of the year, and is observed with more honour than any other festival. Brass bands are borrowed from other villages which are fortunate (or unfortunate) enough to possess them, and the peasants flock in new dresses and bright kerchiefs to walk in procession, pray to the saint, eat, drink, and dance. These feasts are sometimes the occasion of amusing outcrops of the old pagan spirit. Last year, for example, there was a quarrel between the inhabitants of this village, and those of another, further down the valley. When Saint Celestina's day came round, therefore, our people determined to spite their enemies, who honoured Saint Celestina as their special protector. Brass bands were borrowed, fireworks bought, a huge balloon manufactured, a ball arranged for the evening; no pains were spared, in fact, to render the feast so attractive that even the protection of the saint herself could not draw visitors to fill the purses of her legitimate worshippers.

"But what must the saint have thought of all that?" I said, as my informant was gloating over the clever revenge.

"The saint? Oh, she must have been delighted; she had such special honour that year."

Who can say that paganism is dead in this 19th century? Images, too, and small cushion-like hearts blessed by the priest on that special day, are supposed to be of peculiar efficacy against evil. Without the latter, the so-called *benediction*, no mother will dress her child.

I once asked how the young women were chosen who carry the banner of the Madonna in the procession.

"Oh, they're chosen by lot," was the answer.

"Then it's no particular honour, no reward for specially good character," I remarked.

"But of course it is. God makes the lot fall on the one whom He specially wishes; it's the greatest honour a girl can have."

On St. Nicholas' Day, everyone flocks to a little village called Il Melo (The Apple-tree), which worships the saint as its guardian. The village is perched right on the ridge of a chain of hills, bowered in apple-trees and surrounded by chestnut woods. It consists of eight houses (including the *canonica* or priest's house), and a delightfully clean whitewashed church. Outside the church is a large cross of black wood, which the more rigorous kiss before entering; for it was left them, long years back, as the story goes, by a saint-like friar who journeyed through the land preaching to the people.

The Feast of St. Nicholas occurring shortly before I left Tuscany, I resolved to see what was to be seen, and passed the previous night at a farm-house, which, lying higher than my village, was somewhat nearer to the scene of action. A magnificent thunder-storm rendered sleep impossible, and lit up the surrounding hills with wondrous beauty. The next morning was bright and fresh with dripping leaves and mist-wreathed hills, and I started early for the Melo with a peasant friend and my landlord's son. Our party was soon materially increased, however, for we emerged from the chestnut woods on to the road just as a band of men, with three horses, bound for the same village, were passing the farm-house. They were charcoal burners, and the horses were those poor thin beasts which make their way along impossible roads up and down the mountains, loaded with two great sacks of charcoal. Everything was changed to-day, however. The men were not "in black," as *Punch* has it. They wore clean shirts, and bright ties, and carried their best coats flung over their arms. The horses, also, no longer carried charcoal: a single sack, knobbly with parcels for various farm-houses, or with things to be sold at the fair, lay across the pack-saddle, and was tied down with a rope.

"Get up, Signorina," said my friends. "It's a long way to the Melo, and you'll be tired."

"This last horse is quite safe," said the man, "and there's nothing that can hurt in the sack."

It certainly did not look inviting, but I determined to try, nevertheless. So the horse was made to stand by a stone wall, and up I got; on the wrong side, of course—there was no help for that.

The road was like all hillside roads; now up, now down, now of large slippery stones, now of loose rolling small ones; and when the horse took to making glissades down the former and catching his feet in the latter, I did not find a knobbly charcoal sack, without pommel, stirrup, or bridle, the most pleasant of pleasant seats. However I held on bravely by the wooden front of the pack-saddle, and saved my legs if I exercised my arms and back. A curious procession we must have made, winding through the woods to the music of a concertina with which one of the men intended to provide for the dancing.

When we reached the Melo we found that we were among the first arrivals. In the one street there were two stalls covered with brightly-coloured cakes and sweets; a basket of villainous-looking pears sold by a villainous-looking man; a couple of baskets of figs; and a couple of men with steel-yards selling peculiar wafer-like cakes known as *cialde*. Visitors had not arrived yet, however, and to pass the time we sauntered into the church where mass was going on. Towards the end, a man brought round the collection-box and a plate of bits of round baked dough. My companion took two or three of these, putting his penny into the bag at the same time, and handed me a couple.

"What are they?" I asked.

"St. Nicholas' bread. They have been blessed by the priest. Put one of them outside the window when it rains, and no hail will come. Keep them in your bedroom and you'll never be ill."

The village was beginning to look more lively now, for it was getting near eleven, the time for high mass. The peasant women were resplendent in new dresses made for the occasion; some of them even indulged in velvet trimming and dress-improvers, to the undisguised admiration of the swains, and the envy of their less fortunate sisters. They all wore their gayest kerchiefs, generally of fine silk, tied tightly over their well-pomaded hair. Many of the younger women, too, had huge bows of common ribbon, tinsel flowers, and paper lace, boldly displayed in the very middle of the chest. It would have been impossible to wear them at the neck, of course, for they would have been partly hidden by the chin and the kerchief ends. The young men evidently considered grey the correct thing to wear; but they enlivened it by sticking jauntily into their hat-bands flowers and sprays of tinsel of the most amazing forms and colours. Of course everybody talked to everybody, and I was closely questioned by one old woman after another, as to my nationality, family, occupation, etc., etc.

High mass over, the crowd was speedily sucked in by the various houses, and the most important part of the day's business, the feasting, began. My landlord took us to the house of one of his friends, a keen sportsman who had just returned from the low-lands of the Maremma to settle again in his native place. The phrase "Nature's gentleman," has grown too commonplace for use nowadays; but it is the only expression which gives an exact description of our host. He was a tall, finely-built man, small-flanked, broad-chested, with grey, bushy hair, thinnish brown face, aquiline nose, bright intelligent brown eyes, and a peculiar grace in every movement. One of his two daughters (hard-working girls, both of them) had all his classical ease of motion, and a winning suavity and urbanity of voice and manner, that made one envy the clowns she was addressing. The blood of some superior race seemed to reveal itself also in the fine figure, clean-cut features, and wide intelligent grey eyes shaded by thick black hair, of the youngest son.

Our host told us stories of the Maremma. He had once been a thriving farmer there, so he said, but American competition was proving too much for Italian agriculture, burdened as this last is with heavy taxes; and in the last years of his stay there it had not paid him even to reap the crops: he had let them lie rotting on the ground. He told us, too, of the terrible fever, and the terrible remedies by which it used to be combated. He had had as many as fifty leeches on the pit of his stomach at once, in one bad attack. Then he and my landlord began to relate tales of the experiences of their common shooting expeditions in past times, and our host fell on an incident of quite mediæval colouring. He was travelling once with a friend and his wife, he said, in the days before railroads. His friend was taken ill on the road, and on their arrival at the inn where they intended to pass the night, asked for some broth.

"Certainly not," was the answer; "no broth on Friday or Saturday at my house, however ill you are."

So the poor man said, Well, he would go to bed, and see what rest would do for him. To his horror he found he was to be separated from his wife, who was assigned a room on the opposite side of the inn. He rebelled, saying he was ill and wanted her care; but mine host was inexorable; to-day was Friday, he repeated, and on that day it was the rule, in his house, that the men should sleep on one side and the women on the other.

There were about a dozen people at table with us. The men ate with their hats on, and began by asking for a "very little" of everything. Then the hostesses (the two pretty daughters) would press them, would push meat on their plates by force, would fill their glasses with a struggle, and beg them not to make *complimenti*. They finished by doing full justice to the fare. It was indeed such as to invite justice, being well-cooked, well-served, and with all the appointments of the table clean if very rough. The profusion was truly barbaric. There were seven courses, with fruit and excellent coffee, served after the fashion of the place in glasses, to finish off with. I entertain to this day an astonished admiration for those simple peasant women, who cooked all that dinner without help, who yet found time to go to mass and take a short walk in the village in their best clothes, and who did the honours of their table with such inborn grace, without haste, or flurry, or bustle.

We had scarcely finished dinner when a little girl came to ask me if I would care to hear some improvisation. My companion and I went into a house close by and found a small party assembled round a bright-eyed, good-looking woman. She was said to have "raised the glass a little"—a Tuscan euphemism for having been somewhat assiduous at the wine-flask. She had not drunk enough to make her foolish, but just sufficient to make her sing. And sing she did; *stornello* after *stornello*, composing words and music as she went on; singing with that curious monotonous drawl at the end of the verses, which all visitors to Tuscany know so well. She had a fine voice, and could become quite dramatic on occasion, as when she was describing the thunderstorm of the night before, and how she had awaked to find her bed soaked by the rain. She had to sing in church afterwards, however, and wanted to save her voice; so we left her and wandered into the fields till it was time for mass and procession.

After these were over I sat down at the door of one of the houses to watch the crowd surging on the little open space which served as piazza. Everybody was pushing, laughing, joking, and getting very hot in the blazing sun and the dust. Near me a small acquaintance of mine was shouting himself black over a basket of figs which he was selling, if I remember rightly at ten a halfpenny; further on, the villainous-looking pear-seller was alternately crying his ware and devouring it before the eyes of the people, to prove how good it was; "lying pears" (*pere bugiarde*) the kind is called in Italian, but it was not the pears but the man that lied. The dominant voice, however, was that of one of the "*cialde*" sellers. Upright against the corner of the last house, steelyard in hand, this man had adopted a kind of recitative which pierced the shouts of the others by its more musical intonation:—

"*An'iamo Giovinotti! An'iamo Giovinotti! da quelle buone cialde, O——h.*"[4]

Many of the people went off to a meadow near, to dance to the music of the concertina, and we, tired, hot and dusty, set out on our walk home through the cool, fresh chestnut woods.

A WEDDING IN THE PISTOIESE

BEPPE was the eldest son in a little farm-house hidden among the chestnut woods that clothe the Tuscan Apennines above Pistoia. His younger brother, Sandro, was already married, and it was decided that Beppe, too, must take a wife. Another daughter-in-law was wanted in the house. There really were not enough hands, now that wood must be stacked, fields dug, and fodder prepared ready for the winter. Moreover the chestnut harvest was approaching, and too many girls must be hired unless there were someone else in the family to help with the work. So Beppe, resigning himself to his fate with all the stolidity that breathed from his broad, square-cut shoulders and short bull-neck, set to work to find someone to court. His choice fell on a highly-coloured, energetic woman, well known through all the country-side as an indefatigable worker. He bought her a fairing, had the banns published, and married her in three weeks.

I had been passing a few days in the farm-house, and now received most pressing invitations to be present at the wedding. The guests were first to assemble, at about eight o'clock, in the bride's house; then after a slight refreshment, *rinfresco*, to go all together to the church in the village hard by, and thence to return to the Cavi, Beppe's home, to dinner at about midday.

The bride lived some miles away, in a little hamlet perched nearly on the top of the mountain-ridge. The roads were in many places mere mule-tracks through the wood, and it was doubtful if I could get a donkey.

"Come to the Cavi, Signorina," said Beppe; "sleep there, and come out with us next morning. I'm sure my bride won't be jealous."

I hardly supposed she would; still, I did not accept the invitation.

At five o'clock, therefore, on the eventful morning, a donkey, which had been with some difficulty procured for the occasion, was led round to our door by a boy who boasted the romantic name of Poeta, and off we set: my landlord with his gun across his shoulder; his son, in all the glory of black clothes, bright tie, and heavy watch-chain; a peasant woman who had constituted herself my companion, and myself.

We wound higher and higher in the ever-freshening morning air, between hedges gay with autumn berries, until, just below the Cavi, we halted to await the arrival of the bridegroom and his family. First of all they were not dressed —their new clothes tried them, it appeared—and then the bridegroom had forgotten the ring, and must go back across the fields to get it.

We waited for him by a little lonely shrine under a chestnut-tree. The woods which clothed the slopes of the opposite mountains were still hushed in the cold grey-blue of early dawn. Suddenly the scarped precipices and lonely peaks above them were illuminated, as though from within, by wondrous rose-coloured fire, and hung there like some great glowing amethyst between the cold sky above and the cold woods below. Then, as we continued to gaze, the glorious hope was transformed, and merged into the common life of the new day.

Joined at last by the bridegroom, we had a long but most picturesque expedition up a torrent bed, through rocks and woods of infinite variety. The jokes that enlivened it were hearty, if not too refined. They were the sort of jokes Shakespeare's clowns might have made; and, indeed, it often seemed as if the characters of some old play were come to life, and were moving and talking around me.

The bride's house was reached a few minutes after eight o'clock. It was a small one-storied cottage at the farther end of a higgledy-piggledy hamlet. At the foot of the steps which led up to the door stood a man with a remarkably fine white beard, holding a thick stick in his hand. This was the Guardian of the Bride, and he resolutely refused to let anyone enter. A loud altercation arose; Beppe opened his big green umbrella, and, spinning it round above his head, tried to push by; my landlord tried to force his way with his gun; but it was not till pantomime and dialogue had grown fast and furious that the guardian gave the word, and the bride appeared framed in the dark doorway above us. Her rosy face was shadowed by her white bridal kerchief, and in her hands she carried bunches of flowers, which she smilingly distributed by way of welcome.

The door opened straight into the kitchen, where the *rinfresco* was laid. When my eyes grew accustomed to the darkness, and my ears to the sound of many voices, I found myself surrounded by a crowd of women, who were questioning me, as usual, on my most intimate personal affairs. "Are you married or single?" was the first and all-important question. "Where do you come from?" "When are you going back to England?" The questions followed each other fast and thick, as the women looked at me with strange curiosity written in their eyes. I very soon managed to turn the conversation on to their own family affairs, however; and taking into my lap a delicate, fair-haired child, who looked slight and flower-like indeed in that smoke-browned room and among those sunburnt faces, set them talking with much gesticulation and great volubility of feeling about the little thing's illness. They were afraid she would have been lame. "But she's better now, and will grow into a strong woman yet, *se Dio vuole*," they ended, as, smiling down upon her, they turned away to give their attention to the business of the day.

The whole party, some forty in number, now proceeded to the *rinfresco*. On the coarse, clean table-cloth lay great hunks of excellent brown, home-made bread, each piece about the size of an ordinary loaf. These were eaten with slices of raw ham about a quarter of an inch thick. After the bread and ham appeared huge pieces of *schiacciata*, a country cake made of the ordinary dark flour, flavoured with anise, and put to rise like bread. After the *schiacciata*, small cheeses were produced, and, lastly, piles of wafer-like biscuits (*cialde*). Meanwhile drinking had been going on freely. In the middle of the table stood two gigantic bottles of country wine, while smaller flasks were passed merrily about. When full justice had been done to the wine, a light liqueur called *rinfresco* was drunk out of small glasses, as well as another liqueur, the reverse of light, consisting, we are told, of rum and gin, or rum and brandy.

After everyone had thus turned this "slight refreshment" into a hearty meal, the whole party set out for the church, which was at Rivoreta, a village some little distance off. I was walking ahead with my peasant companion and one of the men. This man had been carefully provided with halfpennies, as to the use of which I was hazarding various surmises. We had not gone many steps before we found the road barred by a rope, over which were hung the brightest of coloured kerchiefs.

"What is that for?" I asked.

"They have made the barrier," was the answer; "the bride must pay to go through."

So the man who was with us, the bride's forerunner, paid a halfpenny, the rope dropped and on we went. This was repeated several times, the barriers forming charming streaks of colour under the overarching trees and against the grey stone of the cottages, until the bride had finally passed from the little hamlet where she had lived her maiden life.

In due time we reached the church, and the ecclesiastical ceremony was performed. As for the civil marriage, the peasant mind still regards that as a superfluity which can be gone through or not, according to the convenience of the parties concerned.

I was much struck here by the good feeling shown by this ignorant, illiterate bride. Beppe's father and hers had had some hot words on the subject of the dowry, and the former had sworn that he would not be present at the wedding. Being an obstinate old man he stuck to his word, though he could not resist the temptation of accompanying the party. Near the bride's hamlet he began to complain of a bad foot, sat down by the roadside, and absolutely refused to go farther. At the church door he placed himself on a stone under the trees, and no amount of persuasion would induce him to enter the sacred building. This incident cast a gloom over the whole proceedings, but the bride was not to be daunted. When she and Beppe, now man and wife, came out of the church, she went straight up to him, took his two hands in hers, kissed him, and looking pleadingly up at him, called him by the pretty Italian name "Babbo." The old man was mollified, and walked back much more cheerfully than he had come; though we have since heard that his vindictive obstinacy (a strongly marked trait in the peasant character) was by no means conquered, and that much ill-will exists between the two families.

Rivoreta is a delightfully clean, breezy hamlet, consisting of about half a dozen houses, a whitewashed church, and an airy *canonica*, opening on to a small piazza, paved with white cobble stones. The snowy whiteness of the buildings and the pavement, throwing up the bright colours of the women's kerchiefs and dresses, the whole shut in by embowering chestnuts, formed a picture not likely to be soon forgotten.

The ceremony over, the guests repaired to the one wine-shop of the place to consume more wine and rum; and as this and the priest's breakfast (for Don Tito was going with us) took some time, it was getting late ere the long procession started for the Cavi. First went two women with large round baskets on their heads; this was the bride's trousseau. The bride and bridegroom should have followed next; but as the donkey resolutely refused to play second fiddle, and the way was long, etiquette was thrown to the winds, and we moved on in a merry, haphazard crowd. As soon as the meadow that lies between the woods and the Cavi was reached, however, the bride and bridegroom headed the procession, both with hanging heads; he sheepishly playing with the cheap watch-chain he had bought at the fair, she trying to carry off her embarrassment by smiles, making heroic efforts to be natural in her words and movements.

Beppe's mother was "discovered" watching at the door of the farm-house. She now came running across the field with outstretched arms, according to prescribed custom, welcomed her new daughter-in-law with a kiss on both cheeks, and led her into her new home.

It was now midday. A man-cook and a woman-cook had been hired from the village below and were already hard at work, but the tables had been put before the house on the threshing-floor, and were in the sun; besides, there was not enough room at them, for more guests had come than were expected, and numbered altogether quite fifty. So everyone set to work to help, the tables were carried behind the house on to the grass in the fretwork of light and shade under the chestnut-trees; planks were added to make them longer, and before long everything was ready for dinner. I should not like to say of how many courses that dinner consisted, nor how much the peasants ate and drank, but I know that, of everything that was provided, there was not a crumb of bread left.

The bride and bridegroom were of course placed at the head of the table. She tried to assume an air of indifference; he to make up for his want of appetite and to prime himself to face the assembled company, by assiduity at the wine-flask. Signs, in fact, were not wanting that, however much the marriage may have been originally one of convenience, the passion which sleeps in blood warmed by Italian sun and enriched by the odours of the forest, had been thoroughly roused by the events of the day and the pungent jests of the guests.

I was placed next to the bridegroom, between him and the sharp-faced, humorous-looking priest, and from this coign of vantage could survey all the table. Our friend with the white beard distinguished himself especially; continually interrupting himself, however, to cry *"Viva gli Sposi!"* Then the whole company would clap their hands and cry *"Evviva gli Sposi"* in their turn; only there were some who complained that Il Rosso (the man had been red-haired originally) seemed to have a spite against them, and always called the *Evvivas* just when they had their glasses in their hands.

But he was sly, this Rosso. He would call *"Viva gli Sposi,"* and set the whole table clapping vigorously, and then add as an after-thought, "and the one who married them," or, "and the one next the *padre*"; whereupon Don Tito or myself would have suddenly to leave off clapping, drop our eyes with all due modesty, and thank the assembled company.

Towards the end of the dinner Il Rosso began to hum.

"Will he improvise?" I asked the priest.

"No doubt he will, both he and his father are noted for it; but not yet, he has not raised the glass often enough."

After a little while, however, Il Rosso, feeling himself sufficiently well primed, came to the head of the table. Silence was proclaimed, and he sung a *stornello* in honour of the bride and bridegroom, wishing them the usual good things of this life; children to help them with their work, and plenty to eat and drink. He was followed by a little excitable woman with a strident voice, much admired by her audience, who had already sung once at the bride's house during the *rinfresco*. Her one form of dramatic action consisted in thumping the table with her closed fist.

Dinner being over, a few of the favoured guests were invited into the parlour to take coffee—coffee with rum in it, that is; black coffee alone is not approved of. The rest lounged about the fields and chestnut woods for a time, but by about five most of them were on their way home. They all came and shook hands most heartily as they went away, with a:—"Do come and see me"; for they are most hospitable people, and would beg you to share their last crust of bread with them. *"Vuol favorire"* is the phrase you hear from child or grandmother, if you happen to drop in on them while they are eating.

The guests, having cows and heifers to be seen to before nightfall, set out home through the cool of the chestnut woods; and we, with our donkey and its poetical driver, quietly dropped down the rock-paved road, past the acacia hedges to the village below. The beauty of rock, forest, and torrent had passed into our souls, and I thought wonderingly of the strange mixture of the idyllic and the realistic in the scenes of which this nature had been the setting; of the frankness mingled with reserve, open-heartedness with shrewdness, hospitality with a tendency to critical carping that form the characteristics of this most attractive peasant population.[5]

OLIVE-OIL MAKING NEAR FLORENCE

THE sky, "stripped to its depths by the awakening North," is of that peculiarly limpid clearness which only the *tramontana* brings with it; the sun's rays, penetrating with their full force through the pure, dry atmosphere, are as warm and genial as those of Eastertide. Yet it is mid-winter, and we are going to witness a thoroughly winter occupation; the making of the olive-oil in a villa at a little distance out of Florence.

Leaving the tram at the foot of the hill, we climb for about three-quarters of an hour through vineyards in which the fresh green of the springing wheat contrasts hopefully with the knotted, bare vine branches. The slopes around us are clothed with olives, whose grey-green is thrown into relief by the austere rows of cypresses in the distance, and the spreading tops of the pine-trees on the further hills.

At last, on a ridge between two valleys, we sight the square twelfth-century tower of the villa in question; the remainder of the building dates from the fourteenth century. The heavy grating of the lower windows, the picturesque archway leading to the square, paved courtyard, the little garden on one side, with its olive-tree bending over the grey wall towards the road below—all breathe an almost cloistered quietness. *Parva domus magna quies*, [6] runs the legend sculptured in black letters on grey marble over the house door.

Nothing clashes in this villa. The present proprietor, with his antiquarian and artistic tastes, and his love of Latin inscriptions, has produced a rare welding of past with present. On one side of the entrance gate, for instance (whose columns, be it noticed, are crowned with two bombs, probably French, from Elba), another inscription, unearthed during the excavation of some Roman villa, offers rest to those who are justly indignant at the world's perfidy:

> jovi hospitali
>   sacrum
>
> o quisquis es dummodo honestus
>   si forte
>
> pessimos fugis propinquos
>   inimicorum
>
> solitaria succedens domo
>   quiesce.[7]

The same pessimistic note is struck by a third inscription over the archway before mentioned. There we find, writ large, the following Elban motto:

Amici, nemici;
Parenti, serpenti;
Cugini, assassini;
Fratelli, coltelli.[8]

We owe it to the owner to add that, like most people who rail against mankind in general, he is very tender-hearted to mankind in particular.

Passing from the brilliancy of the outer air, we stumble through a low doorway, over which, on the usual grey marble, stands printed *Frantoio* (crushing-house), and find ourselves in the hot, heavy atmosphere of the oil-making room. We distinguish a low, broad archway dividing the room into two parts, and at the further end a small twinkling light; while nearer the entrance a lamp, swung from the roof, enables us, after a little practice, to make out the objects around us. The whole place is pervaded by a grey steam, sweetish yet piquant, of the peculiar odour of the undried olive.

So great is the heat that the peasants are working without coats, and we, too, are glad enough to lay aside our winter wraps. Looming white through the steam, the first object that attracts our attention is the ox that patiently turns the great stone crushing wheel. Round and round he goes, triturating the dead oak leaves that make his path soft, while the olives, continually poured into the circular concavity in which the wheel moves, are quickly reduced, stone and all, to a dark-looking pulp. The whiteness of the steam and of the ox, the creature's lustrous eyes as they catch the light, the dark olives pouring into the trough, the peasants dimly visible, make up a scene likely to remain impressed for a long while on the memory.

As soon as the crushing process is over and the ox led back to his stall, a number of flat, circular baskets are brought, made of rope-work, and open above and below. The lower openings having been closed for the moment, by drawing a rope, the baskets are filled with the pulp and piled one above another in the press. Now begins the second part of the operation, which costs the peasants a considerable amount of exertion.

We had noticed, near the archway, a tall pole, with a rope round it, pierced by a crosspiece, and turning on a swivel. This rope having been wound round the beam that works the press, and again round another upright on the further side of the press, four peasants set to work at the crossbar. Again and again is the press-bar drawn to the further upright, let go, and drawn back again, while the oil flows in an invisible stream through the pipe that leads to its destined receptacle, which is concealed under the floor beneath a trap-door. Every now and then the men stop and sit down on stones or on a heap of unused baskets to mop the perspiration which streams from them in that warm sweet atmosphere. It was during one of these pauses that they drew my attention to the advantages of the system on which they were working. In other villas, they said, the press-beam was wound towards the peasants, and sometimes broke under the pressure and injured them; but their *padrone* had invented a method of winding it away from them, thus freeing them from all danger in case of a breakage.

Meanwhile, at the further end of the room, by the dim yellow light of the twinkling lamp we had already noticed, another man is busy shovelling a rich dark-brown substance into bins against the wall. This is the so-called *sansa*, the olive pulp from which the oil has been expressed. "It goes down to Galluzzo (the township at the foot of the hill)," said the man, in answer to my enquiries. "There they treat it with sulphuric acid, and get machine-oil out of it."

At last the pulp in the network baskets is pressed dry, the press is unscrewed, the fresh *sansa* shaken out ready to be shovelled into the bins, and the various utensils that have been used plunged into the boiling water of the cauldron that steams in one corner of the room. The trap-door is now raised, and the oil carried across the yard to another room, the walls of which are lined with huge red terra-cotta vessels kept carefully closed. Into one of these the oil is poured and left to settle, *sansa* being heaped well up round the vessel to maintain a high temperature within. When the oil is finally poured off it is of a lovely golden colour, as clear and transparent as water. But it is not destined to reach the public in this Arcadian state. Scarcely has it left the hands of the peasants, before it is manipulated and adulterated to such an extent that even in Florence pure olive oil is almost unobtainable. Cotton oil, colza oil, etc., are mixed with it, rendering it absolutely hurtful to the consumer. The Italian government has offered prizes for the discovery of a method of exposing the adulteration. At present no more certain way has been found than that of Professor Bechi, a well-known Italian chemist. He treats the oil in question with nitrate of silver, and judges of the adulteration by the resulting coloration.

And now, business being over for this week, we are free to go and sup with our peasant acquaintances. Crossing a second courtyard, round which stand houses and stables for the donkeys and oxen (Italians do not work with horses), we pass under a second archway and enter our friend Ciuffi's picturesque kitchen. The rough, uneven stone floor, that looks as though it might have been washed last year, the stout nondescript table, the chairs loaded up with every kind of extraneous matter, the picture of the Madonna with the tiny lamp burning before it, the rows of gaudy crockery over the sink, the cat purring contentedly in the chimney-corner—all these are illuminated, harmonized, almost glorified, by the caressing light of the huge wood fire, whose flames dance and crackle under the great projecting chimney. And beside the fire sits Ciuffi's youngest daughter Armida, a girl of that fair, refined type that occasionally asserts itself startlingly among these black-haired, swarthy-complexioned peasants. She is sitting holding the frying-pan over the fire, but the menial occupation is forgotten as we watch the delicate poise of the head and stretch of the arm, the exquisite Greek profile, the lustrous dark eyes gazing dreamily into the fire, the fair wavy hair coiled into a knot at the back, and the soft pink of the common little cotton kerchief, which, tied with the point under the chin, is thrown up by the dark dress, and sets off the spring of the graceful neck.

And when, the rough white cloth being spread in the visitor's honour, the family cluster round the mediæval oil-lamp that makes a little ruddy blot in the darkness beyond, we are more than ever struck at the wonderful ease and good-breeding displayed in word and movement by these peasants who do the hardest work and live the roughest of lives. The women especially have something indescribably lady-like about them, as they sit eating contentedly, perhaps without any plate, or pass from one to another one of the pocket-knives which are the only cutting implements on the table; or, it may be, question "my man," as to the length of time that will be needed on the morrow to gather in the olives from a certain part of the *podere*. The more one has to do with these Tuscan peasants the more constrained does one feel to adopt the cant phrase, and call them emphatically Nature's aristocracy.

A TUSCAN FARMHOUSE

Of all my experiences among the Tuscan peasants of the Pistoiese, none, perhaps, was more thoroughly characteristic than a three days' visit at a farmhouse just above the village I was staying in. I had just returned from the woods with my hammock, and was feeling rather listless in the absence of my peasant companion, when the farmer's wife, who happened to be in the village that day, said to me, half joking, half in earnest:—

"Come home with me to the Cavi, Signorina; come and sleep there tonight."

I jumped at the proposal, borrowed a big kerchief from my landlady, put a few things into it in the most approved peasant fashion, and we started off together.

I had already been to this farm with some friends for a picnic. On that day the people were threshing and treading the straw; and the stone-paved *aia* or threshing-floor before the house was bright with the corn, and resonant with the sound of the flail. Then, when the sun's rays were less strong—for the peasants only thresh in the bright sunlight—two cows and a donkey were produced, and led round and round, knee-deep in the straw, to break it up for their winter food. I had been much struck at the time by the extreme primitiveness of the labour, though I could not help confessing that the swinging flails, yellow corn, and lazily moving animals formed a very much more picturesque contrast to the low grey stone house, and the blackness of its three open doorways, than any threshing-machine could have done.

Nothing of the kind was going on, however, when my hostess and I emerged from the chestnut woods on this cool September evening. The farmer, just back from his digging in the fields,—there are no ploughs,—was taking a meditative walk in front of the house.

He came forward to meet us, accompanied by his two dogs, and welcomed us with much hospitable grace. One of his sons was near him, watching the two cows graze, and at the same time lazily stripping chestnut leaves for the creatures' fodder off a heap of boughs he had cut. While I was chatting to father and son, my hostess disappeared, and presently came down again, dressed in an old petticoat, chemise, and untidy slippers. She took up a basket of potatoes, and we both set to work to scrape and slice some of them for supper—town people could not possibly eat potatoes baked in their skins, she thought. As we chatted she suddenly exclaimed:—

"See how nice it is to live in the country, Signorina!"

"Why?" I asked, curious to hear what poetical thought had been seething in her brain.

"Well, in the village, you see, you have to wear a dress, and go all clean and tidy, with boots on, too; but here one can go about so nice and dirty."

She had evidently expressed her inmost soul, for she repeated, looking round at the blue hills, and inhaling the cool, fragrant air:—"So nice and dirty one can be here."

By this time it was getting towards twenty-four o'clock. Twenty-four o'clock is a movable hour, and depends solely on the sun. In the height of summer it is at eight o'clock, and then retrogrades by a quarter of an hour at a time till it reaches five, when it begins to advance again. At the end of September, when I left, *le venti quattro* were at half-past six. The peasants' supper-time is regulated by this sliding-scale, much to the disturbance of the appetite of those who are accustomed to eat by the clock and not by the sun.

"Now come and help me cook the supper," said my hostess, as we moved towards the house. "See how many fine drawing-rooms I have," she continued, with a smile.

With that she threw open the first room, and we entered the *metato*. This is the drying room and storehouse for the chestnuts. The floor is of earth, stamped hard. Above one's head, stretching from one side of the room to the other, and forming a sort of ceiling, are narrow strips of wood, laid loosely side by side. On these the chestnuts are piled just as they come from the woods, and the heat and smoke of the fires which are lighted on the floor beneath, penetrating through the interstices, dry the chestnuts and split the shells. From the *metato* we passed through a door on the right into the second "drawing-room," the kitchen. This, as usual, was a large, low, raftered room, with a small window and a big hearth. This kitchen boasted a chimney, however, which carried away, at any rate, part of the smoke; and, more wonderful still, there was at the back a tiny scullery, with sink and plate-racks. For my host was a rich man; not only actual possessor of his farm, but owner of another *podere* higher up on the mountain-side. Passing to the right again, and crossing a small entrance-hall, now full of sacks of grain, we entered the drawing-room *par excellence*, the room in which the family have their meals. This room was nearly filled up by the huge wooden table; but there was still room for a large cupboard with glass doors, behind which the best crockery was displayed, while on the walls hung bad portraits, offered for my careful inspection, of various members of the family. A dozen low wooden steps led from the sacks of grain to the upper regions. These consisted of four bedrooms, the plank floors of which gaped so widely that one could see and hear everything that went on below. Everywhere, in *metato*, kitchen, hall, parlour, and bedrooms, were coloured prints of the Madonna or of some saint; and each bedroom contained, in addition, a little glass box, enclosing a wax baby, surrounded by tinsel flowers. For this is a devout family, fond of processions and tapers. The mother lights a lamp before an image of the Madonna every Saturday; and she told me, with delight, how she had prayed to a certain saint when her daughter's baby was born, intimating that that was why the child was such a fine one.

Our business lay now, however, in the kitchen. It was already getting dark, but a fire was blazing brightly on the hearth, with a copper-lined cauldron suspended over it from a chain in the chimney.

"We are going to have *maccheroni* this evening," said my hostess. "I rolled them out before I left home this morning. But we must cut them first," she added, as she produced the long strips of home-made unbaked paste.

We accordingly cut them into pieces about an inch square, and then, taking a pile in our hands, threw them one by one into the boiling salt and water of the cauldron. While they were cooking we made the tomato sauce, and the farmer grated the cheese; and by the time these were ready, and the table laid, the *maccheroni* could be taken off the fire.

It was now quite dark, the only light came from the dancing flames; and the whole family, including the broad-shouldered shepherdess, assembled in the kitchen to watch the progress of events. By the side of the fire sat the daughter-in-law, a beautiful, fair-haired, refined-looking woman, unswaddling her baby; in the middle of the floor, lighted from the right by the fire, my little grey-haired hostess was kneeling in front of the cauldron and fishing up the *maccheroni*, which she put in layers into a huge red earthern pipkin; and on the other side of the cauldron was the farmer with the tomato sauce, some of which he poured into the pipkin as each layer was completed, adding cheese, pepper and salt. Then there were the two sons, Beppe, low-built and square-cut, and Sandro, the baby's father, more slender, more courteous in manner, but also more lazy; and lastly, two dogs and two cats who prowled on the outside of the group, in eager expectation of their supper.

The *maccheroni* being now all transferred to the pipkin, the water was given to the dogs and cats, and we went into the parlour to eat. Needless to say there was no dressing for dinner. The men came in their hats and shirt-sleeves, the women in their bright kerchiefs. Yet certain rules of etiquette were strictly observed. The system of *complimenti*, for instance, was carried to an extent that seemed ridiculous to English eyes. The mother would fill the son's plate, he would declare he could not eat so much, she would continue to press him, he to refuse, until the voices grew quite loud and excited. When it came to serving the shepherdess, things came almost to a good-natured quarrel. She was a low-built, broad-shouldered, broad-backed girl of about fifteen, of almost gigantic strength, who strode along in her hob-nailed shoes as though she had the seven-leagued boots on. I was evidently a great novelty to her, for she could scarcely eat for looking at me, and presently set the table in a roar of laughter by coming out with a:—"No, thank you," instead of the usual blank "No." Opposite to me sat Sandro with his wife and baby. Charming indeed was it to see the way in which the young fellow fondled and nursed the little one. When he came home from the fields, the first thing he did was to take it in his arms, and sit down on the doorstep in the sunlight; at supper-time he neglected himself to play with it and feed it. There is a great fund of kindness in the Italian character, crossed, however, by a vein of strange hard cruelty, arising perhaps from a remarkable want of dramatic imagination. Sandro and his wife sat side by side according to old-established custom. When a son marries, his housekeeping amounts to this: a double-bed and a large cupboard are put into the biggest bedroom, and husband and wife sit next each other at table. If there are several married sons, all the families live together until the quarrels are so intolerable as to drive them apart.

After supper, at about a quarter past eight, all the family went to bed. Three of the four bedrooms opened out of each other, and in the smallest of these three, the middle one, was a single bed in which the shepherdess usually slept. This was now reserved for me. The bed, the Madonna, and a rickety chest of drawers, were the only furniture considered necessary. In the room on the right slept Beppe and Sandro; in that on the left, which one entered through a doorway guiltless of a door, were the shepherdess and Sandro's wife, Maria. Everyone was in bed in half a minute; for it was summer-time, and they "slept like beasts," as my hostess put it, without even saying their rosary. "Good-night," called out Beppe and Sandro. "Good-night," answered everyone else, and then there was silence till between four and five next morning.

It was hardly dawn when Sandro's voice was heard:—"Emilia, Emilia." The shepherdess gave a grunt, tumbled on to the floor, and a moment later strode fully dressed across my room, clamped downstairs and went out. Maria slept longer, for the baby had kept her awake. As a matter of fact, the little thing could scarcely be expected to sleep, for it had been kept under the bedclothes all day. Italian peasant-babies have not a very pleasant life of it. In the morning they are tightly swaddled, put into bed under a wooden frame, and entirely covered with the clothes. There they lie in the dark, sleeping or screaming till about midday when they are taken up, reswaddled, fed, and put

72

to bed again till the evening. Then the same process is repeated, and they are expected to sleep all night. This particular baby was washed about twice a week, if indeed the term "washing" can be applied to the operation. The mother sits down by the fire, and puts a glass of wine by her. She then fills her mouth with wine, puts it out into her hand, and rubs the baby, which screams violently.

At about eight o'clock the men came in from the fields, the cauldron was suspended from the chain, water was boiled, and my host set to work to make the *polenta*. The maize flour is added gradually to the boiling water until the mixture is so thick that none but a strong man can stir it. Then it is turned out on to a board kept for the purpose, cut into slices with a string, and eaten smoking hot with cheese. There are no plates, of course; all stand round and help themselves. Maize flour, chestnut flour, lentils, cheese, and beans, are the staple food of the peasants, with now and then a fowl to celebrate some specially great *festa*. Milk they never seem to drink, butter they rarely make; they use their dairy produce exclusively for cheese.

These Tuscan peasants may be called an industrious race; that is to say, they are never entirely idle. At the same time they do not work in such a way as to make it tiring to watch them; they take things very easily. A strong, well-built man, for instance, will be contentedly stripping chestnut-leaves off the branches for the cows, or leaning against a tree watching the animals feed. In another part of the field a woman will be taking advantage of the gusts of wind to *folare* her grain, that is, to complete the winnowing of it. She spreads a sheet on the ground, empties a sack of corn on to one corner of it, fills a heavy wooden tray with the grain, puts it on her head, and turns to catch the wind. As soon as she feels a gust—*folata*—she lets the corn fall in a narrow trickling stream on to the sheet; the chaff is blown away in the descent, and the winnowing is completed. The very poor have a terribly hard time of it, however, for they do the work of mules and donkeys, carrying great loads of wood on their backs for many miles over the hills; and no one thinks of mending or making roads for them. An old woman I was once talking to told me of the huge burdens she used to carry in her youth.

"The roads were bad then," she said, but added naïvely, "they are better now; they were mended for the horses."

But to return to my hosts. On Sunday morning, the day being a *festa*, the house received its weekly apology for a sweep, the women put on dresses and kerchiefs, and went so far as to comb their hair, and we started for the village, to go to Mass. It was very picturesque to watch the parties of rosy, healthy peasant women as they came along the road, in their bright aprons and head-gear. In one party was Beppe's intended bride.

"Come to Rivoreta, and see me married, Signorina," said she. "Do come."

And with many promises that I would do so if possible, I took leave of my kind friends.[9]

THE FLORENTINE CALCIO: GAME OF KICK

WE may not approve of the manner in which Italy is living in her Past, and celebrating centenaries when she ought to be setting her face strenuously towards the Future; nevertheless, we must confess that the Florentine fêtes a year or two back presented one historical spectacle that was distinctly worth the trouble of reviving. We refer to the mediæval game known as *Calcio*, or Kick, which is interesting to English and American youths as bearing at least a superficial likeness to Football. At the time of the fêtes it was indeed spoken of as the Football of Florence; but it differs from Football in two ways that are eminently characteristic of Italian character: it is more complicated and more spectacular.

To begin with, there were twenty-seven actual players needed on each side, besides trumpeters, drummers, standard-bearers, referees, and a ball-thrower. Of the twenty-seven players, fifteen, divided into three equal companies, were placed face to face with the enemy in the front of the battle, and bore the brunt of the strife. They were called Runners (*Corridori*) or Fronts (*Innanzi*).

Behind the three battalions of Runners were placed in loose order, extending across the whole breadth of the field, five Spoilers (*Sconciatori*), so called because their business was to spoil the game for the Runners of the opposite side.

The Spoilers were supported by four Front Hitters (*Datori innanzi*); and these again by three Back Hitters (*Datori indietro*). These Datori may be spoken of as Half-backs and Backs.

The favourite Calcio ground in Florence was the square before the church and convent of Santa Croce. Here the great costume matches (*Calcio a livrea*) were held, as well as the ordinary games (not in costume) which enlivened the cold afternoons during Carnival time. A description of one of the costume matches at once makes clear the fundamental difference between Calcio and Football.

The field was 100 metres long by 50 broad, enclosed top and bottom by a palisade, on the left by a ditch, on the right by a low wall. Along the wall were erected stands for the more honourable spectators and for the umpires. At each end of the field was a tent round which stood the referees, standard-bearers, etc., of their respective sides, together with showily dressed halberdiers, who were also stationed at intervals round the field.

The spectators being assembled, the umpires and, perhaps, some foreign potentate or his ambassador, seated in the stand above the wall, the grand march in of the players commenced. It was a procession of picked men from the noblest Florentine families. For the Calcio was an aristocratic game. It was not to be played "by any kind of scum: not by artisans nor servants nor ignoble nor infamous men; but by honoured soldier men of noble birth, gentlemen, and princes." The ages of the players ranged from eighteen to forty-five, and they were all well-built, athletic men. They wore light shoes, long hose, doublet and cap, and their costumes were of the most splendid material—velvet, silk, cloth of gold or silver—for were not the brightest eyes of the city to watch the game? Not only did each side have its own colours, but the players had also to be dressed in the same material.

The march was opened by the trumpeters and drummers. Then came the Runners, going in couples, and chequer fashion: a red, say, behind a white, and *vice versâ*. The Runners were followed by nine more drummers preceding the standard-bearers, each dressed in the colours and bearing the flag of his side. Finally appeared the Spoilers, the Half-Backs bearing the ball, and the Backs.

After making the round of the field the procession, at the sound of a single trumpet-blast, split up into its component parts. Trumpeters, drummers, referees, standard-bearers, placed themselves at the tents of their respective sides; the Runners divided up into their companies of five and faced each other in the centre of the field; the Spoilers placed themselves at a distance of 13½ metres behind the Runners and 9 metres from each other; the Half-backs 10½ metres behind the Spoilers and 12 metres from each other; the Backs again 10½ metres in the rear of the Half-backs and 17½ metres from each other.

A second trumpet blast, and the serving-men retired from the field; a third, and the game began.

The Ball-bearer (*Pallaio*), in a parti-coloured dress formed of the colours of both sides, threw the ball with great force against a marble sign let into the middle of the wall on the right-hand side of the field. It rebounded between the two ranks of the Runners, who immediately rushed towards it, acting, however, not independently, but in their companies.

The company of Runners which had possessed itself of the ball began, of course, to work it with their feet towards the opposite goal. Now came the turn of the Spoilers, of whom the two nearest left their stations and ran obliquely at the advancing Runners, hustling them and endeavouring to get the ball from them and pass it to their own Runners, who were hovering near.

The Runners and the Spoilers worked the ball forward with their feet; the Hitters (Half-backs and Backs) were allowed, nay, as their name implies encouraged, to use their hands.

If the Runners succeeded in taking the ball past the Spoilers, they had to face the onset of two Half-backs, who, if they got the ball, would probably pitch it clear over the heads of the players to the Half-back on the opposite side. This was considered very diverting play, and was much appreciated by the onlookers.

Having pierced the lines of the Spoilers and Half-backs, the Runners found themselves opposed by one of the Backs. The Backs were the strongest men on the field, as, being placed so far apart, they were obliged to act separately.

The ball was generally knocked, not kicked, over the goal. When this happened the two sides changed places on the field; the winning side marching to its new position with flag unfurled and waving, the losers with furled flag and lowered staff.

Such is a diagram—a mere diagram, though a correct one—of the Florentine *Calcio*. Its connection with Football evidently lies, to adapt an expression from the vocabulary of folk-lore, in the fundamental formula: to send a ball through a goal without the aid of an instrument. But this formula developed differently in England and in Florence. The traditions of the Florentines were military. Their youths were trained to war from boyhood upward: they were accustomed to act in bands. Has anyone ever noticed the truly military spirit in which Dante continually combines the souls into bands, *schiere*, moving and acting in unison? The remembrance of the disposition of the Roman army, too, with its close and extended ranks, still lingered amongst them. Add to this that they were a thoroughly artistic people, devoted to spectacular effects and cunning in the planning of them, and we at once perceive the cause of the radical difference between this most interesting game of ancient Florence and the English Football.

Those were the times when Florentines penetrated either as merchants or exiles, and generally as both combined, into all parts of the Peninsula and of Europe; and they took their games with them. Matteo Strozzi's sons, one of whom was Filippo, the famous founder of the great Strozzi Palace, more than once beg their mother to put balls in with linen, etc., which she constantly despatched from Florence to her exiled family, these balls being probably for the most energetic game of *Pallone*, still played throughout Tuscany.

They took the *Calcio* with them too, just as the English take their football, cricket or tennis. Thus Tommaso Rinuccini, living at Lyons, writes in his memoirs that: "When Henry III., King of Poland, after the death of Charles IX. his brother, left Poland for France in 1575 to take possession of the kingdom, he passed through Lyons in France. And the Florentines living in that city played before him a *Calcio*, in which all the Florentine nobles took part, as it was their custom to do. And they sent Pierantonio Bandini and Pierfrancesco Rinuccini, two extremely handsome gentlemen and tall, both Florentines (who were the standard-bearers in the *Calcio*), to invite his Majesty, in the name of their native city, to be present at the celebration. King Henry accepted the invitation and was a spectator of the game. When he spoke to them before they left his presence he asked whether all Florentines were as tall and handsome as they."

It would be, indeed, well for the physical development of modern Florentines should the *Calcio* enter again into the ordinary life of the youth of the city.

---

[124]
[125]

ELBA

[126]
[127]

A MONTH IN ELBA

I.

An atmosphere as invisible as that of Egypt, a sea of the clearest amethyst and emerald, merging into sapphire in the distance, and jealously guarded by a series of frowning headlands, now grey, now black, now red, with heart and veins of iron, that enclose miniature beaches and mysterious grottos where the water sleeps peacefully in the arms of its lord; and within, a sea of vines embracing the feet of mountains clothed with pines, with lentisks that have watched the passage of centuries, with bushes of white heather taller than a tall man, with glaucous agaves, rigid and puritanical, with prickly pears, fantastic and repellent; the very air of a voluptuous quality: soft, velvety even, with the mingled odours of an infinite number of aromatic plants and herbs, sweet with the white amaryllis that fringes the sea. Such, in broad outlines, is the island for which Etruscans, Romans, Genoese, Pisans, Saracens, Spanish, French and English have fought, in which Victor Hugo was nursed into life, in which Napoleon was caged; a land of wine and iron, glowing with strength and passion.

A land of perfect peace and infinite possibilities does this island seem as one drifts along the coast, watching the fish dart below the keel of the boat, rounding the islets that look as though they had skipped from the mainland in play and were intent on their own reflection in the water; as one swims into grottos purple-roofed, over water of the purest aquamarine, and looks through the narrow opening across the twinkling sea outside; or, as one walks through miles of vineyard in which grow the choicest grapes, or climbs up to the iron quarries, where the mountain is being simply dug away.

Yet, the deepest impression made on the mind of a visitor to Elba is not so much that of the future prosperity of the island, for all its resources, as of its past importance. Almost every peak bears its ruined castle; headland after headland was fortified in the Middle Ages by Powers jealously tenacious of their rights; the iron quarries, now comparatively little known, were worked unremittingly by the ancients, witness Virgil's well-known line:

"Insula inexhaustis Chalybum generosa metallis;"

and witness the iron slag that proves the existence in Roman times of furnaces for refining the ore; the very wine, delicious as it is, is no longer the great source of wealth it was some years ago, partly on account of the phylloxera which has lessened the production, partly because the customs-war between Italy and France stopped its export to the country which afforded the most profitable market, partly for the reason that the peasants are primitive enough to insist on selling the unadulterated juice of the grape to a public that prefers manufactured wines.

All this adds to the sense of repose; the past is so long past, the future seems still so far off. And meanwhile the peasants and the small proprietors prune their vines and shell their almonds, and use their old-fashioned lamps, and dance barefoot on *festas* to the music of a concertina, either at their own houses or at the *palazzo* of a neighbouring large proprietor. They give each other nicknames, which gradually supplant the surnames, descending from father to son after the fashion of primitive times. Thus a man who thought a good deal of himself was called *il Papa* (the Pope), whereupon his sons and sons' sons are called *Papini* (little Popes); a man noted for his patience was called *Giobbe* (Job) and his children are known as *Giobbetti*; a man who once wore a coat that was too long for him has ever since been called the Doctor; another from a bad stroke at bowls rejoices in the name of Scatterer (*il Baracone*), and one who should now call him John would be scarcely understood. They intermarry largely. They troop from all parts of the island on donkeys and diminutive horses to the *festas* of the various miraculous Madonnas, not omitting to go down to the nearest beach on the eve of a *festa* and wash according to traditional custom. They preserve local differences and hostilities that tell of difficult intercommunication: thus a Lacona man will tell you that the men of Capoliveri,[10] whose township he can see perched on a hill to the east, are "*danniferi*; what they have with their eyes they must also have with their hands," he adds, as he picks up a bunch of unripe grapes, wantonly broken off and thrown away. No one but a Capoliveri man would commit damage of that sort.

The earliest among the buildings that tell of the past importance of the island is the Castle of Volterraio. A ride along the hills overhanging the gulf of Portoferraio brings us to the foot of the precipice on which it stands, rising, with the sheer rocks that form part of the building, out of a tangled mass of low growth, from which, every now and again springs a graceful wild olive. By only one path is the place accessible. Path is a courtesy title. The way up is a scramble, often on hands and feet, up smooth, slippery, slanting masses of jasper rock in whose crevices flourish rounded, hedgehog-like cushions of the most cross-grained thorns. Ten minutes' climb brings us to an ancient wall with a gap, where was once a gate, and a strongly built, vaulted guard-house. Up again, over short grass this time, and we come to the low, narrow doorway at the top of a steep flight of steps sheer down on one side, without any trace of railing. At the bottom of the steps a hole in the ground gives evidence that an upright there supported a further defence of some sort. Inside, where armed men fought, a couple of fig-trees flourish greatly, and the ground is a series of heaps of grass-covered *débris* that sound strangely hollow as one stamps on them. The sentinel's round within the castellation of the walls is still intact. At some little distance on each side of the tower, which forms the south-eastern corner, it stops short, and deep holes for uprights in the parapet show clearly that a drawbridge on each side enabled the defenders to isolate the tower and fight to the last gasp. At one place it widens out. A number of men could make a stand there; the inner wall is pierced with many loopholes, and these all converge on one place: the steps leading up to the wall, and the well at the bottom of them. One can creep too, into a number of dungeon-like recesses in the walls, or clamber through a hole down a steeply inclined ledge of rock to a little underground chamber having a recess like a rough bed on one side, lighted by a hole in the rock that forms the roof, and another in that which looks over the gulf. A small opening, defended by an outwork, puts this underground cell into communication with the outer world; but the outwork is evidently a comparatively late structure.

All this is absolutely lonely, save for a few goats that now and again make their way up, and the falcon that screams and wheels overhead. Once it was the storehouse of the Etruscans of Volterra, who, drawing iron, copper[11] and other minerals from the island, built the Volterraio as a defence for themselves and their treasures in case of sudden assault. It has stood many sieges, has heard the oaths of many nations in Roman and Mediæval times and is now falling to decay; for Turks and Saracens roam the seas no more, and the island it helped so long to guard has become part of a united peaceful kingdom.

Quite the most curious proofs of the ancient importance of the island are to be found between the little villages, of S. Ilario and St. Piero di Campo, overlooking the southern coast. We are in a granite country from which the stone is exported for sculptural and architectural purposes. No need of quarries to obtain it, though; it lies scattered over hill and valley in huge blocks, as though some prehistoric giant had dumped cart-load after cart-load with the idea of raising some enormous building, but had been cut off by a god in the midst of his operations. They have a certain defiant air about them, still, those masses of granite. They shrug a shoulder at you from under the houses, they poke out a rounded back in the very middle of the church wall, they lie across your path in winking, slippery masses, nourishing thorns in their bosoms on to which you may fall, and then, if you look up suddenly, you may see one that has climbed on to the shoulders of his brethren and with feathered cap stuck awry, and big empty eye-sockets, is grinning down at you with unholy, sardonic mirth. Every little fold in the hillside, shut in strangely from the outside world, has its chestnut grove and its running stream; but even here there is something uncanny, and no peasant will put his lips to that water without making the sign of the cross above it; he fears he may become possessed by the spirits that haunt it. It is curious, however, that if he takes the water in a glass he considers himself free from the danger.

In the midst of all this weird desolation rise two Roman buildings at some little distance from each other; one a spacious ancient church, the other a square tower. They are built of beautifully hewn blocks of granite, oblong or square, but mostly square, at the surface, put together without mortar. The door of the church is low and square, not arched; its face is pierced just under the roof (now fallen in) by a rounded window formed of smaller slabs of stone, also without mortar, in which a bell formerly hung, but which does not give one the idea of having been built for a belfry. The building is rather oblong than square, and was apparently divided into two unequal portions by a low granite wall, which does not seem to have much in common with an altar-railing—it is too much towards the middle of the church and appears to have been altogether too strong a construction. The apse is extraordinarily shallow, pierced by three of the loopholes that at long intervals serve as windows to the church. There are no traces of pillars.

At some distance from the church the granite rocks have piled themselves into a peak that looks straight over the underlying plain to the sea beyond. On this peak stands the tower. "The solidity of its walls," writes that most conscientious, but not very critical historian, Giuseppe Ninci,[12] "the smallness of its rooms, the great difficulty of access, show it to have been one of those terrible prisons in which pined for long years those unfortunates who, exiled from their native land, were sent off to the islands." If prisoners were put there, it must have been to starve, and for that they might surely have been shut up in some place which would cost less to build. There is but one side on which it can be approached, and even there a man must twice grasp the edge of the rock above his head and draw himself up by sheer force of biceps before he reaches the base of the tower. Once there he discovers that he must repeat the operation, for there is no door, only a window above his head, which he can reach by stretching up his arms. The tower consists of two low rooms one above the other, with walls a metre thick. Was it really a prison, or was it not rather a watch-tower, or a tower of refuge? Otherwise what should it be doing there all alone on its granite base? Was there once a Roman or an Etruscan city round that large church or temple? Yet, the huge granite blocks look as though man had never attempted to oust them for his advantage. Wanted, an archæologist's report before these writings of past history become still further obliterated.

St. Piero di Campo is well worth lingering in for a while on one's return from San Giovanni. It was always a favourite landing-place for hostile ships, the plain below being fertile, and the gulf sheltered. The castle, therefore, contained everything that could be wanted in case of siege: a church, and a graveyard in addition to the usual means of defence. It is a square, massive building, with but one small entrance. The church is extremely ancient. The roof, low and vaulted, is supported on two short, thick granite columns, one having a roughly carved capital which is well worth study, the other none at all. The walls have been barbarously whitewashed, but in two or three places where the whitewash has been chipped off, there stand revealed the figures of early 15th-century frescoes executed by a Tuscan artist. One or two figures have been laid bare as a matter of curiosity, and it appears probable that the whole church is frescoed in the same way. If so, and the Campesi would undo their barbarism, it would be worth a pilgrimage to see.

II.

SURELY no city in the world queens it over the waves so completely as does Portoferraio. She rides them imperiously, lifting high the turrets that are her crown and defence; she decks herself in the brightest colours, conscious of her beauty; and sets herself boldly on the very head and front of the dark blue waters that wash her feet or leap up in wrath at her pride, yet never injure her. Genoa is called the Superb, but the epithet rises more spontaneously to the mind on view of the capital of the Island of Elba.

Portoferraio was originally one of those headlands, so characteristic of Elba, that grow out from the mainland on a narrow stalk, and then widen and heighten into rocky peninsulas. It is now, however, an island, for Cosimo I., Duke of Tuscany, cut a moat through the stalk, and severed the peninsula from the mainland. The peninsula consists of two heights, on one of which is the fort known as the Falcone, on the other, that of the Stella; and these are bound together by a lofty wall, within the castellations of which sentinels could walk without descending into the town. Immediately below each fort, a bank of concrete, kept in former times very clean and free from growth, formed a water-shed for the rain which streamed down it into a cistern below. At present the concrete, though still railed in, is quite overgrown, for the city boasts a water-supply brought down from the neighbouring hills. Round the forts are spacious granite-paved squares on which considerable bodies of men could manœuvre; and below cluster the red-roofed, green-shuttered houses, whose inhabitants sleep, in Oriental fashion, through the heat of the day, coming out in the evening to walk among the oleanders of *Le Ghiaie*—a tiny park above a beach of the whitest gravel (*ghiaia*)—or to dance with the officers in the new bathing establishment, of which they are so proud. Down again, at the foot of the houses, lies the port, a semi-circle pointed at the southern end by the pink-washed tumble-down offices of the sanitary inspector, at the northern end by the octagonal tower of the convict prison. Soldiers, convicts, "society," trade, all hive on those two little hills, and the only opening through which workers and drones can pass in and out on the landside is a low-browed gateway, bearing the Medici arms, and overlooking a plank bridge spanning the moat of sea-water. Within the gateway is a wide, open space, through which one passes up the first ramparts of the Falcone, to a wonderful winding tunnel, hewn in the solid rock. This brings one out through another gate, into the flaunting little city. The tunnel is known as *La Tromba* (the trumpet-shaped), and was the work, as usual, of Cosimo's engineer.

Portoferraio, Ferraio, the iron city, as it was originally called, dates, at any rate, from Roman times. The name would suggest this, and the fact is abundantly proved by Roman walls, pavements of brick and marble, tombs with inscriptions, skeletons, lamps, etc., coins of consuls and emperors, workmen's tools, that were unearthed from time to time during the seventeenth century, when excavations were being made for the subterranean cisterns, guard-houses, powder-magazines, halls of every kind that honeycomb the ground.

Towards the end of April, 1548, there arrived in the bay below Portoferraio a fleet bearing one thousand soldiers, three hundred sappers and miners, and the architect John Baptist Camerini. Ferraio was at that time a heap of ancient ruins, but Cosimo I., the merchant Duke of Tuscany, whose coasts lay open to the invasion of the Turks, and whose galleys were continually assailed by pirates, concluded that the best possible points of defence against these redoubtable enemies were Ferraio and Piombino. With a large sum of money, and a very great deal of diplomacy, he persuaded Charles V. (who thought that the same points of defence would be as irritating to the French as to the Turks) to grant him the places. The agreement was hardly concluded when the Duke's men landed on the little peninsula, quarried the blocks, ready squared to their hands from the Roman villas and walls, made a brick kiln on the coast near by where there was suitable clay, obtained excellent mortar from the stones of the neighbouring hills, and in a fortnight had raised the walls breast high. Cosimo made two visits to the island to inspect the works, living not in Ferraio itself, but in a house on the hillside opposite, that is still known as the Casa del Duca (Duke's house), and bears on its garden wall a defaced, weather-stained marble bust of Duke Cosimo. The Turks, the French, the Genoese, and the rest of Cosimo's many enemies were beside themselves with rage. Elba was wasted throughout its length and breadth, the new town—no longer Ferraio, but Cosmopolis—was besieged by mighty fleets, intrigues were obstinately kept up to induce the Emperor to revoke his grant, but the Duke (now Grand Duke) made head against force and intrigue; the town remained in his hands, and still, as witness to his might, bears over its gateways the proud inscription:

templa, moenia, domos, arces, portum,
cosmus florentinorum dux II. a fundamentis
erexit an. MDXLVIII

The port, as made by Cosimo, still remains, but the defences and engineering works completed by him and his successors are now deserted, or have been turned into the convict prison, the three white columns of whose water-gate form a striking feature in a view of the port. The convicts are here allowed to work at various trades. Workshops are provided within the prison walls, and a show-room for the sale of their goods. The government exacts a small royalty on objects sold.

A sentimental interest attaches itself to Portoferraio, as being the place which preserved to mankind a sickly puling infant of the name of Victor Hugo. An epigraph by Mario Foresi, on the walls of the town-hall, commemorates the fact.[13]

Along the shore of that part of the gulf, which lies outside the port, the sea looks as though some eccentric gardener had been laying out garden beds in it, with grassy walks between, and white pyramids at irregular intervals. These are the *saline*, where the government makes salt (not very good salt either) for its subjects. It produces about 1,152 tons a year, which it sells at the rate of *3d.* per pound. Truly a government salt monopoly is not a pleasant thing for peasants, who can get salt alone as a condiment for their soup of cabbages and beans, or their mess of maize flour.

Ferraio, then, takes its name from the principal product of the island, but the mines are not near the town; they are on the eastern coast, at Rio and at Cape Calamita (Loadstone Cape).

Rio, like all other villages in this part of the world, consists of two parts: Rio Alto, whose streets are merely a succession of stairs; and Rio Marina, a modern town, where the mines are. The prevailing colour in Rio Marina is red: red are the hills that shut out the fresh north breezes from the town, red is the sea where the steamers lie off to be loaded, red are the four piers where the trucks go up and down, red the houses, with their curtains, stairs, and furniture. This red ochrous ore is associated, as one ascends the mountain, with the massive and micaceous varieties of hæmatite; so that while one sees red cliffs towering on one side, and solid knobs and blocks of iron, almost native, on the other, one walks over roads that glitter and sparkle like running water, and are almost as slippery as ice.

> "And Seius, whose eight hundred slaves
> Sicken in Ilva's mines,"

writes Lord Macaulay; thereby showing that he had never been to Rio. For there is no mining properly so-called here; there is no tunnelling, no blasting on a large scale. The men work in the open air, digging away the red earth, blowing away the harder masses with small charges of powder or getting them out with picks. The earth is washed in a large cistern, with a revolving paddle-wheel, that keeps the water in continual motion; and the iron thus separated from the clay is loaded on to the ships without further refining.

At present the mines are farmed out by the Government, and produce about 176,516 tons yearly. The men are paid by piece work, and earn from two francs to four francs a day. Only one set of men is kept. When they are not lading foreign vessels, they dig ore, and make great heaps of it; when they are not digging, they lade. It is evident the place wants development.

At the iron quarries of Cape Calamita, where magnetic iron is obtained, we watched the process of lading. A large English-built steamer had come in, under a Genoese captain, for iron, which it was to exchange for coal at Cardiff. She stood in as near to the shore as was safe, and then anchoring, opened three mouths on each side to receive her food. Come out to her six willing slaves, small boats called *laconi*, with the most audacious masts and yard-arms one can imagine. They look as though they would rend the clouds and pierce the sky; but it is all bluster; the boats are such helpless creatures that if they are to cross the bay, they must have a steam-tug to pull them. The men in the *laconi* rest planks on the open lips of the monster that towers above them, and proceed to pour down its six gaping throats an infinite number of small baskets of the red, earthy ore. For four consecutive days they feed her, if the weather be fine, and then she goes off to the northern seas, where *laconi* are unknown, where the water is rarely motionless, and where steam cranes and puffing engines tell of work done in a hurry. It must be confessed, however, that the Elban method is adorably picturesque. Sea, sky, and hills are glowing in the great calm. The big black ship lies motionless; her crew lounge, her jovial, white-suited captain, so proud of his mahogany-fitted passenger ship that used to go to India, stands watching the ore slide in; the Elbans cluster up the sides of the planks to pass the baskets from one to the other; they talk and laugh, showing glittering white teeth; and they wear hanging red fishermen's caps, patchwork shirts and bright sashes.

Onward along the coasts from Rio, we come to the ancient town of Portolongone, built along the curve of a fine, natural harbour. Sheer above the town, where the Portolongone women flaunt it along their sea front after mass, in the brightest of dresses, and the most artistic of black or white lace head-veils, rises one of the strongest fortresses of the island. It was built in

1603, to the infinite dismay and disturbance of such small fry as the Florentines, Genoese, and the Pope, by Philip III. of Spain. The approach to it is broad, but very steep; the outer ring of fortifications are a city in themselves; and within, across the inner moat and drawbridge, there are spacious squares, clusters of houses, an interesting church, and the large prisons in which are kept criminals condemned to solitary confinement. The prisons we cannot enter, but let us sit for a while in the chaplain's cool, brick-paved room, sipping the country wine and breaking the long, curled strips of pastry which his hospitable womenfolk have heaped on the table, and listen to what he has to tell us of his charges.

"No," he says, "they none of them live long, once they come in here; they go mad or fall into consumption, and so die if they have not succeeded in committing suicide first. We have to look out sharply to prevent that. A man managed to do it, though, about a month ago. He tore his shirt into strips and made a slip-knot for his neck, climbed, no one knows how, to the grate in the middle of the deep window-hole, and tied the end of the noose there, bound his own hands together somehow or other, and then kicked away the stool he had been standing on. When he felt himself strangling, he struggled to get free, but his hands were fast, and he only succeeded in pulling the noose tighter and tighter. He was quite dead when they took him down. Outside the prison are a number of cells open to the air, closed by iron gates. You can see them down there." We were walking about outside by this time, where the convicts not in solitary confinement are building the new prisons. "Every prisoner has an hour's turn in one of those open-air cells once a day, guards pacing outside the gates the whole time.

"Their food? Well, yes, as you say, it is clean, savoury, and well-cooked"—we had been peeping into the kitchens as we came along—"but they have a very small allowance; a plate of soup given half at midday and half in the evening (vegetable soup, with *pasta* in it) and two loaves, not much bigger than rolls, of white bread. It is piteous to see how a stout well-built man dwindles away on this *régime*. The men who are at work buy extras with their wages. Those who wear chains from ankle to wrist were sentenced under the old penal code. When they go to bed they are chained to the wall. Chains are abolished by the new code.

"The prison consists of two storeys of cells, running down each side of a central corridor that extends up to the roof. Communication with the cells of the upper storey is obtained by an iron balcony which runs the length of the building at the height of the first storey. All the cell doors open towards the inner end of the prison, where an altar has been set up.

"When I say mass, they are all set ajar (there is in every case an iron gate, kept locked, inside the wooden door), and so the prisoners can look at the altar without seeing each other. I go round to them at regular intervals, unless someone calls for me specially, and talk to them from outside the iron gates. No, I am not afraid, but it is the custom. They generally like to have me go, and appear really to appreciate the comforts of religion. Read! Ah, you saw Library printed up near the gate, did you? But there are very few books in it. What can we give them? They must not read novels, and they must not read politics. I give them a religious paper about the miraculous Madonna at Pompeii, and some of them read that. Otherwise they do nothing. All the work of the place, washing, nursing, cooking, building, cleaning, is done by convicts. Even the barbers are convicts, and as they have nearly served their time, and besides get better paid than the others, they are careful of their behaviour; there is no need to be afraid of them. That house down there, with its back against the rock, is the lowest depth of all. The cells are dark, and none but the most refractory prisoners ever go there. It has been empty for some time past.

"Born criminals? No, I don't much believe in that doctrine; I think that in most cases one whom Lombroso would call a born criminal, may be saved by careful training. Before I came here I knew a man who brutally killed his wife while his little boy looked on. The man was condemned; we looked after the bringing up of the boy. At first but little could be done with him. He would bully his fellows, and then, crossing his arms over his breast, would throw back his head defiantly and say: 'Do you know who I am? My father was the terror of the village.' He did not seem to know what pain was. I have seen him undergo an operation in his finger which had been caught in a machine, without a sign of suffering. One day the lads were working at a machine, and one of them grew tired. 'Who'll take my place?' he called out. No answer. 'Will no one help me?' Another pause. Then the criminal's son called out, 'I will.' He went to the machine and worked there till he was nearly dropping with fatigue. But from that day he was completely changed, and he has grown up into a quiet, trustworthy, hard-working man."

By this time our courteous host had accompanied us back to the inner gateway; and so, taking leave of him, we left that terrible artificial world, over which, with a hush still greater than that of the sea and sky and mountain, broods the awful presence of unknown crime terribly expiated.

THE FIRST STEP OF A MIGHTY FALL

"*Le premier degré d'une chute profonde*," says Victor Hugo, speaking of Elba in connection with Napoleon. And it is impossible to remain in the island long without conjuring up the figure of the fallen prince hurrying hither and thither with one or two attendants, building his villa, enquiring into the agricultural and mineral wealth of his new kingdom, collecting his taxes and his customs duties, strengthening his fortifications, holding the tiny court of which the people of Portoferraio were so inordinately proud, carrying on his *amours*, chatting with the peasants and the proprietors—and under the mask of all this activity enlisting men, collecting stores, conducting a continuous secret correspondence with Naples, with Corsica, with France, undecided whether to make himself King of Italy or to go back to be Emperor of the French.

Elba, towering above her satellites Pianosa, Monte Cristo, S. Stefano, Giglio, with the rocky islet of Palmaiola as sentinel in the very narrow channel towards Piombino, is an excellent place to plot in, and a very difficult place to watch. Napoleon, as was but natural, took in the advantages of his position at a glance. He had hardly arrived in Elba before he claimed the neighbouring islands as part of his domain, and began to establish outposts on them. Thus he surrounded himself with a barrier within which no foreign ship could penetrate without violating the independence secured to him by the Treaty of Fontainebleau; and which at the same time afforded him a valid excuse for short sea-trips and for a constant movement of small vessels eminently adapted to conceal secret negotiations of every kind, and especially his intercourse with Corsica. In this most favourable position, shut off from prying eyes by diplomacy and nature combined, within easy communicating distance on the one hand of Tuscany and of Murat, on the other of Corsica and France, Napoleon remained from May 4th, 1814, to February 26th, 1815. With his political intrigues during that time we do not propose to concern ourselves, nor with the vexed question raised by some disappointed Frenchmen, who seem to have understood neither the Treaty of Fontainebleau nor the geography of Elba, as to England's complicity in his escape; rather we would picture him in the places with which we too are familiar, would shadow him forth not as the banished Emperor of France, but as Monarch of Elba.

By the time the English frigate, the *Undaunted*, that bore him, reached Portoferraio, Napoleon had decided on the line of conduct he intended to pursue: that of a monarch on a small scale, intent on developing the resources of his kingdom, firm in exacting respect for his new flag from all maritime powers. And so well did he play his part of miniature kingship that even Sir Neil Campbell, English Commissioner in the island, thought that he was contented; and more than once opined that if Napoleon were well supplied with money—as he should have been by the terms of the treaty—he would remain quietly where he was; but he was such a very eccentric person that, if he ran short, there was no knowing what improper conduct he might pursue.

He assumed this position at once on his arrival in the harbour of Portoferraio. He refused to land until his new subjects should have had time to prepare an ovation suitable to the reception of a monarch, and he issued an address to General d'Alhesme, then commanding in the island, in the following terms:—

"General! I have sacrificed my rights to the interests of my country, reserving the sovereignty and possession of the island of Elba. To this the Powers have consented. Have the kindness to make known the new state of things to the inhabitants, and the choice that I have made of their island as my abode on account of the mildness of their customs and their climate. Tell them that they will always be the objects of my warmest interest."

The Portoferraiesi took the Emperor at his word. They were overwhelmed with gratitude at the honour he showed them. They received him with flags, with fireworks and with Te Deums; they sent deputations to wait on him; they presented him with a map of his dominions—a very bad one, by-the-by—on a silver tray; they gave up their best furniture to furnish, provisionally at least, the Palazzina dei Mulini, just under Forte Falcone, where he was to live; they took his officers into their homes; they put on their finest dresses and went to receptions in the town-hall in the evening, telling themselves that their city already seemed like one of the capitals of Europe. And Napoleon fostered their delusion. He proposed to readopt the name given to the city by Duke Cosimo de' Medici, and to call it Cosmopoli; deriving the first part of the word, not from Cosimo, but from the Greek *kosmos*, world, declaring that his Cosmopoli was to be the *City of the World*. At the same time he built and altered extensively in and around his house, adding another storey, planting a garden, forming a library, erecting a tribunal and theatre; he shipped over furniture from the mainland; he prepared a residence close to his own for his mother; he bought land and built a country-house not far from Portoferraio; he sent for his sister Pauline; he prepared extensive stabling; he established a lazaretto in the harbour, which was to compete with that of Leghorn: everything pointed to complete acquiescence in his position.

He had, in fact, scarcely landed before he began to take possession of his new dominions, as a good monarch should do, and had soon visited the places of importance in Elba and its dependant isles. His corpulence rendered climbing and even walking difficult, but his active spirit overcame all difficulties; and the Elbans who met him, his officers and attendants, continually on the roads and mountain paths, felt quite convinced that the Emperor was devoting himself to their welfare.

One of his first expeditions brought vividly before him the extent of his fall. He had visited all the forts and surroundings of Portoferraio, had collected information concerning the salt manufacture (a Government monopoly) and the tunny fishery; and turning to the left from the land gate of Portoferraio, had pushed as far as the iron mines of Rio—then, as now, Government property—and the fort of Longone; but he had not yet climbed the hills that shut in his capital at the back. These are crossed by a few bridle-paths and by a road, sheer up and down, paved now with the native rock, now with loose, rolling stones, and known as the Colle Reciso. About half-way up the Portoferraio side of this road, a breakneck path leads to the right, up the face of a hill called St. Lucia, whence the Etruscans once drew copper for their bronze. The Emperor, Colonel Campbell, General Bertrand, and their attendants, riding to the top of this hill, found themselves among the ruins of a very large ancient castle. The towers lie prone in enormous masses of masonry, the walls have partly fallen in, partly been quarried for surrounding buildings; of roof there is no trace; the place is simply a large grass-grown square surrounded by naked, ruined blocks of masonry. Not quite abandoned, either, for in one corner is a tiny church with a couple of rooms built on to it in which a hermit once lived and died. Here the party halted and looked round. They were dominating the narrowest part of the island. Right and left the hills stretch away in barren, fantastic peaks now crowned with ruins, now sheer with granite cliffs; before and behind the sea is visible in four different places. Napoleon looked around for a little while, taking in the principal points of the landscape, and then, turning to Campbell, said, with a quiet smile:—"*Eh, mon île est bien petite.*"

Later on he would often follow the Colle Reciso down into the fertile, vine-covered plain of Lacona, which lies at its foot on the southern side. The conditions here, even now, are truly patriarchal. The mountains form a semi-circle about the coast; and in the midst stands the proprietor's villa surrounded by eucalyptus trees, prickly-pears and aloes—an island among the spreading vineyards. To see the *contadini* waiting at the well for the master, his arrival with his family, and the respectful familiarity with which they take their orders from their *padrone*, is to get a glimpse into old world ways and ideas such as does not fall to the lot of everyone.

From this plain springs the headland known as Capo di Stella. It is narrow and low at its base, but rises and swells as it advances into the sea, and becomes a wild rocky hill, with sheer precipices down to the water, covered with lentisks, with aromatic herbs, with great silvery shining thorn-bushes known to the inhabitants as *prune caprine*. It is the home of hares and innumerable birds. Here Napoleon proposed to make a preserve for game; and actually went the length of arranging matters with the proprietor, Jacopo Foresi, and of making some show of beginning the wall which was to span the isthmus, cutting off the headland from the rest of the estate. Needless to say that the game on Capo di Stella was not in reality profoundly interesting to Napoleon, and that the plan was never carried out. There is an incident recounted of the Emperor in these parts, commemorated by an inscription affixed by the present proprietor, Mario Foresi, to the walls of the house of one of his peasants. A certain Giaconi was ploughing when Napoleon came along, and in his character of one interested in everything, took the ploughshare out of the man's hands and attempted to guide it himself. But the oxen refused to obey him, overturned the share and spoilt the furrow. Foresi's inscription runs as follows:

napoleone il grande
quivi passando nel MDCCCXIV.
tolto nel campo adiacente l'aratro d'un contadino
provavasi egli stesso ad arare
ma i bovi rebelli a quelle mani
che pur seppero infrenare l'europa
precipitosamente
fuggirono dal solco.[14]

Farther along the coast, to the west of Lacona, and separated from it by a semi-circle of almost pathless hills, is the beach and village of Campo, where are extensive granite quarries. To this place also Napoleon paid several visits, and caused a road to be made winding round the base of the hills and joining it with Portoferraio. Must he not develop the resources of his island by providing for the carriage of its granite? Or rather, would not such a road be extremely convenient for keeping up communication with the outlying island of Pianosa, where he was collecting troops and training cavalry? The room where Napoleon passed the night on one of his visits to the village is still shown; an old man, too, blear-eyed and tottering, is listened to with a certain respect by the villagers as he relates how he was nursed and caressed by the Emperor. His father had been a sailor in one of Napoleon's fleets, had been taken prisoner by Nelson, had spent many years in England, had been ultimately accepted as a sailor on an English ship, and had made his escape from Genoa. Napoleon visited the man, made him relate his experiences, and showed himself affable with the children, as was his general way in Elba.

Most thickly do reminiscences of Napoleon cluster round the lovely village of Marciana. The road leading westwards from Portoferraio skirts the seashore. On the left hand rise cliffs densely overgrown with white heather; below, on the right, lies the shore in a succession of bewitching bays and headlands. A ride of between two and three hours brings one to a village lying along a graceful curve, backed by dense chestnut woods, over which hang the frowning precipices of Monte Capanne, the highest mountain in the island. This is Marciana Marina. Behind it a steep, boulder-paved path, running along a ridge above the chestnut woods, where *cicale* sing all day long to the sound of falling waters, leads to Marciana Alta, a fortified place defended once by a huge castle. The castle is now a mere shell within which fowls are penned; they pick up a living among the heaps of *débris*, and drink out of the two halves of the large iron crown which once hung proudly above the Medici arms. To the right of Marciana Alta, a long Via Crucis leads to a church known as the Madonna del Monte. The road is absolutely breakneck, formed of blocks of stone, which devout visitors to the shrine have hammered into the soil at their somewhat eccentric pleasure. The church is one of the richest in the island, possessing beautiful massive silver chalices and lamps, rich vestments, vineyards and fields. It stands in a wood of magnificent chestnut trees, and has at the back a charming semi-circular wall of grey stone, divided by pilasters into three sections, each of which contains an ancient stone mask spouting the coldest, lightest of water. Close by the church is a little house in which a lay hermit lives. What wonder that Napoleon should take a liking to so picturesque a place, renowned throughout the island for the excellence of its air and its water? What wonder that he should love to retire thither, and to wander through the woods to the truculent little village of Poggio that stands up so defiantly on its granite prominence? That he should even like to picnic on the road in the fold of the hills where the five springs keep up a continuous splashing? That he should choose this place to receive that mysterious lady (in reality, the Polish Countess Walewsky) whom the unlucky mayor of Marciana wanted to fête as no less a person than the Empress Marie Louise in person? Surely all this was harmless and natural enough. But follow up the path that leads off to the right of the hermitage, pass out of the shade of the trees and across the granite boulders to the promontory that commands the coast of Elba, the mainland, and Corsica. There two huge masses of rock tower above their comrades. Between them is a little stairway, partly natural, partly artificial, which leads to the top of the outer rock. This presents a natural platform shielded along part of its length by a natural parapet. The parapet has been added to with brickwork, and a deep hole big enough to hold a large flagstaff has been driven into the platform. This was a favourite resort of Napoleon's. What place could be better for taking the air? And what place could be better for signalling to Corsica, the window-panes of whose villages glitter at so short a distance? As a matter of fact it is some thirty-five miles away; but in the limpid atmosphere of this "isle of the blessed," distance, like time, seems to be annihilated. Here then, like the hero of Balzac's tale, would the prodigal sit gazing at his *peau de chagrin*, now so wofully shrunken, and scheming for some way to reverse the spell and restore it to its former amplitude. Vain dream! from which he was finally awakened by the rude shock of Waterloo. After Napoleon left the island, the people of Marciana put up a pompous inscription on the outer wall of the church. It runs as follows:—

napoleone I
vinti gli imperi
i regi resi vassalli
da rutenici geli soprappreso non dalle armi
in questo eremo
per lui trasformato in reggia abitava
dal 23 agosto al 14 settembre 1814
e ritemprato il genio immortale
il 24 febbraio 1815
da qui slanciossi a meravigliare di se
novellamente il mondo.

il municipio di marciana
con animo grato e riverente
a tanto nome
decretava di erigere questa memoria
il 18 febbraio, 1863.[15]

Of regular residences Napoleon may be said to have had three in the island of Elba: the Mulini in Portoferraio, the country-house at St. Martino, and a house at Longone. The Mulini is a small, two-storeyed house, with a garden behind it, and a winding path leading down to the sea; the path ends in a little grotto known as "Napoleon's bath." The Emperor occupied the lower storey, giving the upper one, which he himself had built on, to his sister Pauline. No trace of the illustrious occupant now remains: the furniture has been entirely removed, some of it, as in the case of a bed in my possession, having left the island altogether; even the library, presented by Napoleon to the town, and lodged in the town-hall, has been to a great extent scattered, owing to the carelessness of the municipal authorities. Only one tangible record of the Emperor remains: the bronze mask in the chapel of the Misericordia. Antonmarchi, Napoleon's doctor, made in Paris three bronze masks from the plaster cast which he had taken immediately after the death in St. Helena. One of these masks passed through the Murat family into the hands of the sculptor, Hiram Powers, in Florence, and is now[16] exposed for sale in London. The second I have not been able to trace. The third is at Portoferraio, kept in a handsome sarcophagus, and exposed to the public gaze every 5th of May, when a funeral service is performed over it. The face, as shown by the mask, is thin and drawn, the brow heavy and projecting; the likeness to the bust of Julius Cæsar in the British Museum is quite extraordinary.

Napoleon's country-house at St. Martino lies in the fold of the hills west of Portoferraio. The building of it enabled him to play to perfection the *rôle* he had determined to adopt. He bought up the ground from the small proprietors who owned it, respecting, however, the rights of one old woman who refused to sell; and as soon as the works were well under way was continually to be seen riding along the road from Portoferraio to inspect their progress, supervising everything, chatting with everybody, talking to the children and giving them money. A tree is still shown which he is said to have planted with his own hand. Round the house, which was quite small, is a wood with fine old ilex-trees through which a path leads to the spring at which Napoleon loved to drink, and to the right rises a hill which the peasants still call the *hill of sighs*, because, they say, Napoleon used to go up there to sigh for his beloved France. The Emperor's bedroom has been preserved intact, with its pretty decorations and its charming Empire furniture. Near the bed are two windows, of which one, just at the level of the eyes of a person lying there, opens on to a superb view of Portoferraio, the sea and neighbouring coast-line.

The house within the fort at Longone is now as bare as that at Portoferraio. The place, however, is interesting, for it was with the excuse of repairing the fortifications there that the Emperor supplied himself with guns and ammunition; while the ostensible sale, at Genoa, Leghorn, and other places, of the old iron found in the fort, afforded him an additional means of communication with the Continent. He was very frequently at Longone while maturing the final details of his escape.

Notwithstanding his apparent affability towards the Elbans, intended, we must believe, rather to mislead outsiders than the people themselves, Napoleon was not popular in the island. Being in continual want of money he was obliged to tax the people beyond their resources; and they naturally saw clearly that, whatever he might say and however condescending he might show himself, the money he drew from them was by no manner of means applied to the improvement of their position. His tax-gatherers were insulted; riots took place in the very churches when the priests gave out the date by which the taxes were to be sent in; in one village troops were billeted on the inhabitants until the last penny should be paid. The cries of "*Vive l'Empereur!*" which had originally greeted him on his various expeditions, ceased to be heard.

Before matters reached a veritable climax, however, Napoleon had played out his part, and had left the island in which he had landed with so many fine promises. He had shown himself a clever actor, a skilful intriguer to the outside world of European diplomacy; debauched, tyrannical and exacting to the inner Elban world, into which foreign diplomats could pry with difficulty. In his vices, in his astuteness, in his ambition, Napoleon, as he revealed himself in the island of Elba, moves backwards through history, and takes his place beside the Borgia, the Orsini, the Medici of the fifteenth and sixteenth centuries.

Of the caricatures of the period the most interesting is the grimly ingenious German portrait of the Conqueror, to which the following explanation is attached: The hat is the Russian eagle which has gripped with its talons and will not leave go; the face is composed of the bodies of some of the thousands he has sacrificed to his ambition; the collar is the torrent of blood shed for his vain-glory; the coat is a bit of the map of the confederation arrayed against him and of his lost battlefields. On his shoulder, in the guise of an epaulet, is the great hand of God, which plucks the cobweb and destroys the spider that fills the place where a heart should have been.

FUGITIVE PIECES

[166]
[167]

A TALE FROM THE BORDERLAND

"WELL, it is a story to take or to leave. I tell it you as it happened to me. Think what you like about it."

The speaker was a spare man of middle height; an Anglican priest, whose long black coat and white band set off a face that might have belonged to a seer of old: pallid yet not bloodless, with delicately cut mobile nostrils and grey eyes now piercingly bright, now losing themselves in far-off mystery. The few grey hairs combed across the ample brow seemed instinct with the life beneath them. In moments of great spiritual excitement, when the eyes kindled and the nostrils worked, they would appear to rise as into a halo above the inspired pallor of the face. And the cypresses were around us, gloomily aspiring; while the ground on which we sat was alive and gay with the most delicious little pink cyclamens: sweet, everyday human thoughts that come like a smile across the over-strained soul.

"I was in England then, working in a large Northern parish in the midst of dirt, misery and ignorance; and would often come home exhausted by the sufferings I had seen and could do so little to alleviate. One pouring wet evening I got in very late, soaked to the skin, faint with hunger, oppressed by the thought of the preparation needed for an early communion service I was to celebrate on the morrow. I told Janet to admit no one: that for no reason would I go out again that night; and sat down to dinner.

"I had hardly begun when the door bell rang, and voices reached me from the hall—that of a woman, evidently a lady, pleading, and Janet's, repeating my order.

"'But,' the strange voice insisted, 'he would surely come if he knew. It is to see a dying man. Tell him it is to see a dying man. To save a passing soul.'

"The woman's distress and anxiety were so evident that I could remain passive no longer. I called Janet and told her to show the lady in. She was tall, graceful, dressed in black, with a long veil which she kept lowered, so that I could see the features but indistinctly. With every sign of agitation she repeated to me what she had said in the hall. 'Would I come with her? It was to see a person who must die this night, and all unprepared.'

"I had no heart to refuse; and we sallied forth together, she leading, I following. After some time I found myself in a better part of the town, where the rows of squalid houses had given place to detached residences, each in its garden. At one of these we stopped, ascended the steps, and I rang.

"The door was opened by a butler, who had the air of being an old, confidential servant. I asked to see the person who was dying.

"The man looked at me in amazement. 'No one is even ill here; much less dying. You must have the wrong address.'

"I looked around for my mysterious guide. I was alone.

"'But,' said I to the butler, 'I assure you that a lady came to me this evening, asked me to follow her to a house where a man must die this night, and led me here. Are you certain there is no one ill?'

"'Not only my master, but all the servants are perfectly well,' was the reply.

"Just then a door opened and the master of the house appeared: a young, florid man, easy and good-natured, with a certain air of distinction about him. I introduced myself and repeated my story.

"'Well, come in out of the rain now, at any rate,' said he. 'I am just sitting down to dinner. You will not refuse to join me?'

"I accepted the invitation and found my host bright, well-read, well-travelled: a most agreeable companion.

"As we were smoking after the meal, he said, hesitatingly:—

"'Do you know I have been wanting to make your acquaintance for a long time past? I have had an instinctive feeling that I could confide in you as in no one else: a strange sympathy going out to you while you were personally unknown to me. And now I feel it stronger than ever. I cannot shake it off. May I make a father confessor of you? I am sick of this life. I want to be at something real.'

"I encouraged him to speak, and promised him all the help my experience should enable me to give him.

"'Well, I will leave you for a little to collect my thoughts,' said he. 'Be so kind as to remain here.'

"While he was away I looked about the room, and found myself attracted by a picture, evidently a portrait, of a lady. I considered it attentively, and to my utter surprise recognised my mysterious visitor and guide.

"'Who is that?' I asked my host on his return.

"'That? My mother. She died when I was a child. Yet'—with a hesitancy that was almost shamefacedness—'yet, I feel somehow as though she were still caring for me.'

"We had a long talk in which he recounted his life, that of a young man about town; and the upshot of it was that he promised to come to the communion service on the following morning.

"I was at the church very early, waiting anxiously for his appearance.

"'Do you really suppose he will come?' said the friend who was to help me celebrate, and to whom I had related the strange experience. 'You had better give up any hope of seeing him. It was probably nothing but a fit of the sentimentality that follows a comfortable dinner. It took that form because you happened to be with him. I have seen dozens of such cases.'

"Still I had faith in my convert; and as the service went on and he did not appear, I felt my heart grow big with sorrowful disappointment.

"I walked home sadly enough.

"In the hall I found the butler of the previous evening. He looked white and scared. He was trembling.

"'Sir, sir,' he stammered, 'come with me. Come quickly. My master is dead. I found him dead this morning.'"

A silence fell upon us. The cypresses waved mysteriously towards the heavens—my friend's face, with the awe-struck eyes, showing white amid the gloom.

"A mother's love," he murmured. "Why should it not compel the forces of material being? A mother's love. Is it not 'the last relay and ultimate outpost of Eternity?'"

THE PHANTOM BRIDE

THERE were three of us: men between youth and middle age who had gone through school and college together, had walked the hospitals and worked in the dissecting room without a break in our friendship; and, separated by the exigencies of our practice, had still, as though by some occult sympathy, kept in touch with each other across long stretches of absence and silence. We were sitting with our coffee and cigarettes on the public walk above Florence. Before us lay the great square with the colossal David: the bronze giant that looks ever to the hills beyond the town, with his sling ready to defend her from assault; while behind us rose the church from which the creator of that giant really had protected the city against the strange-speaking North-men who had poured over those very hills for her destruction. The last gleam of sunshine was, as we knew, making the gold of the mosaic glitter over the church-door there above us. It lay too on the town at our feet, lighting up the captivating grace of the bell-tower, the chastened glow of whose marbles seemed actually before our eyes; bringing out the unsurpassable curves of the cathedral dome, and the squatter lines of that of St. Lorenzo, where the Medici moulder in their marble tombs; lingering on the graceful sturdiness of the Palazzo Vecchio; touching the spires of the church of St. Croce and of the Bargello where prisoners once pined. It was that hour before the actual sunset when the city, lying languidly amid the encircling hills, seems consciously to breathe out the suavity by which she captures her lovers and holds them to her in life-long thraldom. And two of us had been long away from our mistress; the spirit of the time and the place was upon us; confidences of loves and sorrows rose naturally to our lips.

Conti flung away his cigarette and threw himself back in his chair. I glanced at his small nervous hands as he folded his arms; remembering their quick, sure movements in the most delicate operations; and then I looked into his blue eyes, whose bright sparkle the deadly habit of morphine-taking, the future ruin of that bright career, was already changing into dreaminess.

"Decidedly, Neri," exclaimed he, "you are the most changed of the three. There you sit smoking your cigarette as quietly as though we came here every day of our lives. With a line between your brows, too! You look as though you were obliged to take a wife to-morrow. What has happened? Has someone got drowned in such a way that you cannot tell whether it was a homicide or a suicide, and are afraid of misleading justice? Has a supposed corpse come to life again and objected to being dissected?"

A smile flickered across Neri's gravity. He was the handsomest of the three: one of the best made men in the town. He wore a thick, pointed beard, and the mouth under the moustache was of quite exceptional firmness and delicacy. In fact he was what the women call a *bell'uomo*; and but for his thorough-going solidity of character and immense variety of interests, would infallibly have had his head turned by their admiration. As it was he simply had no time to give them very much attention. And lately, so we were told, he had taken less notice of them than ever; but had gone about his work with the line between his brows, and lips that rarely relaxed except to smile encouragement to some poor patient on whom he had operated.

He breathed out the smoke slowly, luxuriously, from his mouth and nostrils—he was a confirmed cigarette smoker—and answered:—

"No, I am not going to be married to-morrow; and I was thinking of a *post-mortem*, but not of such an one as Conti imagines. I will tell you the story; but keep it to yourselves. There's a woman in the case, of course," he added, with a short nervous laugh. Then he hesitated again, and at last began.

"Just a year ago to-day I had to make a *post-mortem*, and a report to the police, on the body of the one woman who has entered profoundly into my life. She was a rising operatic singer with a singular power of vivid dramatic intensity, though I do not think her impersonations were ever a full expression of her innermost powers. Her interests were extremely varied, her mind exceptionally mobile—her occupation fostering this mobility, and increasing that power of quick sympathy, of putting herself into touch with the people with whom she came into contact, which was one of her distinguishing features. She was not beautiful; but she had fine large dark eyes that looked straight at you; and she was so lithe and girl-like in all her movements (she was rather older than myself in reality) that you felt inclined just to take her in your arms and hold her fast against all the troubles of the world—and she had her share, I warrant you."

"H'm," said Conti. "And you did it, I suppose. You seem to have been hard hit."

"No, I did not do it; although I was more than hard hit. Her position was so difficult that I had no heart to make it worse; and she had a certain dignity about her, even in her moments of most childlike *abandon* in talking with me, that prevented any light advances. You felt as though you must help her even against herself, for her nature was evidently passionate; and that made your feeling for her all the more profound. She had married unfortunately; a man who had ill-treated and neglected her in every possible way. After a couple of years she fled from her husband, left the stage, and changing her name, lived by giving singing lessons; and, when I first knew her, was making a brave struggle not only to support herself and her boy, but to obtain and hold such a position in the world as should enable her to launch him in his career. Then she fell ill; more from exhaustion of vital force than anything else; and I never saw anything like the spirit with which she bore up. She was almost too weak to teach, and held her pupils together with the greatest difficulty; yet she managed always to wear a bright smile, and she refused absolutely to give up hope. 'Why, it is the most stimulating of medicines,' she would say. 'If I give up that, I shall collapse immediately. I consider that, given the conditions in which I live, self-deception, on the right side of course, is a distinct duty.'

"Towards the end of the summer she left town for a fortnight, and I went out to see her. She insisted on our having a little picnic together, and took me to the top of a hill hard by. There was a small pine wood up there, with a stretch of grass and ling. Opposite rose Castel di Poggio. The hills were round us ridge on ridge, and fold on fold; their bosoms veiled by draperies of mist, for it was still early. We might have been hundreds of miles away from any town: yet Florence was close at our feet. I had left it only a couple of hours ago, and should be down there again breathing the phenic acid of the hospital that same afternoon. Never shall I forget the morning of chat and reading (I had taken up a volume of poems—her gift), with the bees booming in the ling, the gorgeous green of the pine needles, intense unchangeable, against the brilliant sky, and the mingled scents of pine, cypress, honey-flowers, and aromatic herbs. As we were starting to go down she stopped. 'We must keep vivid the remembrance of this, Neri,' she said, and caught my hand. I turned and looked into her eyes, whose deep earnest gaze remains with me yet. We clasped hands, and so parted.

"Well, when she came back to Florence she began to lose her spirit. Money matters worried her, I fancy, though she would never trouble me with them. Then her husband accidentally found and began to trouble her, threatening that unless she went back to live with him he would take the boy (now nearly seven years old) from her. She sent the child to her people in Switzerland. 'It would so much simplify matters if I were to die,' she wrote me once. 'My people would never let him go then; and my husband could urge me no longer. The struggle is too great. Only I do not want you to have to make the *post mortem* on me when I have said good-bye to this life: it would be too painful for you.' Still I did not think she would ever really commit suicide; not because she had any fear of death, but because I knew she looked on the proceeding as cowardly; and also because she had a power of the most intense enjoyment and interest in all the beauties of life, whether physical or intellectual. Hers was the most elastic nature I have known. I said what one could say, and it's precious little, in such circumstances: and she seemed to recover tone.

"Then I left Florence for nearly a month. I was obliged to return unexpectedly to the hospital; and was just leaving it to call upon her when I was told there was a *post-mortem* waiting for me. I went into the room. It was she; lying there on the table....

"Well, I got through somehow. It did not take very long, for I knew her well enough to guess what she had used, and had only to verify a suspicion. And while I was working it seemed as though she were looking at me, looking at me with a pitifully pleading look as though supplicating forgiveness for the horror of my position. I remember I kept her covered as religiously as though she had been alive; and I remember I arranged everything when all was over and carried her in my own arms to the bier which was to take her away. Then, I believe, Paoletti found me, got me into a cab, and drove me home in a high fever. The second evening I came to myself. I was without fever and fell quietly asleep. Towards morning I awoke. She was there standing by my bed with the same pitifully pleading expression I had felt in the hospital. She caressed my cheek, then bent over me and touched my lips.

"Oh yes, I know. *Optical hallucination, subjective sensation*, and all the rest of it. *Hallucination*; *subjective* as much as you like; but I saw her; and I feel her about me now just as plainly as I felt her then. I suppose the impression will fade as time goes on. I may take a wife and have children as other men do. Still (with a repetition of the little nervous laugh) it has not begun to fade yet; and I feel as though I should see her once more: on my death bed."

*   *   *   *   *

"Decidedly," said Conti, breaking the silence. "Nature's irony is more scathing than man's. It is just Neri,—- Neri who never philandered, who never sentimentalised, who would have nothing to do with what was not downright brutally real—it is just Neri whom the Fates have wedded to a phantom bride."

"Come," said Neri, shaking himself, "it's nearly dark; we can see neither dome nor bell-tower any longer. Shall we go to the Arena? Tina di Lorenzo is acting. And then we will finish up at the Gambrinus Halle."

CYPRESSES AND OLIVES: AN INTERLUDE

Amice, quisquis es, dummodo honestum, vitae taedet.

THE road was parched and burning. I was sad, so sad, at my heart's heart. The sun seemed to laugh me to scorn, and the passers to sneer as they went by. My soul was sore, sore to its inmost fibres, and I hated the very beauty of Nature.

So I turned aside among the cypresses. They will calm me, I thought. Their whisperings are so grave. They flaunt not their joy at the sun's kisses, like the shameless trees along the roadside. They keep their hearts unmoved in sun and in storm; they are the true stoics of Nature. And their calm is sympathetic; it comes not of a soul immovable; it comes of strength in trial.

And the cypresses wrapped me round in their scent—the grave, penetrating odour in which the battered spirit folds its wings to rest, and the heart-beats grow quieter, and the brow smooths itself out in peace. In long, long lines they stretched away before me, and I walked under their guidance, conversing with them familiarly, searching the height and depth of their thoughts. And I was no longer sore with my fellow-men. I could tolerate the thought of the flaunting trees and flowers, of the exuberant life evermore renewing itself away out there along the road I had left. But still I walked among the cypresses, and with them I held communion.

And lo! they took leave of me. At the edge of a grassy path they left me. And beyond the path I saw freshly-ploughed brown earth, and the quiver and strain of a yoke of white oxen as they pulled the plough through some harder spot; and two workers with brown aprons, arms and faces like glowing bronze, and soft felt hats weather-stained into harmony with the earth and the tree-trunks. They bent to their labour; and the soil laid bare its breast, rich in promise, before their eyes; and the vines around whose roots the plough passed encompassed them with luxuriant clusters, purple and white; and the olives bent close down around their heads, embowering them under a low roof of silver. So I passed through the toil of those workers, toil calm and regular, blest in its fulfilling and in its ending; and I carried in my heart the picture of those bending men, the slow-moving oxen, the rich soil and the embracing trees.

Suddenly a spell was woven round me; a spell as of moonbeams. I was in a wood of olive trees. Their sharp, narrow leaves, of a sheen like frosted silver, pointed with rigid grace into the luminous grey of the sky. No shadow, no darker spot of black or green fruit broke the wondrous diffused splendour. The very branches, as they spread and bent outwards from the low trunks, had softened the harshness of their scaly bark and were as softly radiant as the foliage and the sky above them. Only the trunks and the under-sides of the branches were in shadow; rugged and brown, they were like a rough shell which had opened to give life to an Aphrodite of new and chastened beauty. No flowers jarred with bright tints the harmonious hush of colour; but here and there delicate campions raised slender stems that bent with the weight of grey-green calyx and pallid, wide-eyed blossom.

And I walked, in the exquisite suavity of the wood. Surely, I thought, the moonbeams have become tangible. Surely I am in an enchanted land and should meet its mistress; a maiden slim and grave, with wealth of olive-black hair, with deep dark eyes, with clinging gown of grey girdled with a zone of cold blue-green. How sweet to stay here for ever with soul attuned to the melody that mutely breathes from the living silver of boughs and leaves, and falls graciously from the pearl-like sky.

But onward and ever onward must I go; and the olives left me as the cypresses had done.

They left me at the edge of the highway; and I passed out again into the glare of the sunshine, the gaze of the passers, the laughter, the bustle, the pushing, on the parched and burning road.

And behold! a change had come over my soul. The stoicism of the cypresses, the calm of the toilers, the suave quiet strength of that harmonious olive wood—these things had permeated the fibres of my being. The indifference of the passers-by found no way open to my heart; the unheeding joy of trees and flowers no longer jarred me. I was clothed upon with a vesture woven of the enduring calm that broods ever at the unchanging heart of Nature; like armour it encompassed me about, and I possessed my soul in peace.

LOVELORNNESS

AFTER THE MANNER OF THE EDDA

BALDUR was once obliged to go away out of Asgard and leave Nanna all alone. So Nanna was very sad. She knew that no one would hurt her Baldur, but still it was to her as though he had been swallowed up by the mists of Niflheim, and as though she would never see him again. So she went to the Norns who dwell by the tree Ygdrasil, and she said:—

NANNA: "Tell me, oh Norns, who know all things. What can the body do, when the soul has left it?"

NORN: "The body when the soul has left it can do nothing; it is lifeless and inert, and turns to dust."

NANNA: "Tell me, oh Norns, who know all things. What can the thoughts do, when the master-brain has left them?"

NORN: "The thoughts fly hither and thither when the master-brain has left them. They seek their director, and finding him not, fall fluttering to the ground lifeless and useless, or lose their way along paths that have no ending."

NANNA: "Tell me, oh Norns, who know all things. What can the eyes do, and the ears, when the lord they love to see, and the voice they love to hear, have gone from them?"

NORN: "The eyes grow dim with watching and longing, and the ears deaf with hearkening and listening—nought else can they do."

NANNA: "Tell me, oh Norns, who know all things. What can the limbs do, when the support they twine round has been removed?"

NORN: "The limbs fall powerless to the earth when their support has gone; they cannot raise themselves nor stir themselves; they await a wakening voice, which shall bid them live once more."

NANNA: "Tell me, oh Norns, who know all things. What can the heart do, when the body is lifeless, the thoughts scattered, the eyes and ears worn, the limbs powerless?"

NORN: "The heart is no longer in the body. It went away with the soul, with the master-brain, with the lord the eyes loved to see and the ears to hear, with the support the limbs clung to. And not till that great awakening lord brings back the heart, will the body become quickened, the thoughts reach their mark, the eyes and the ears revive, the limbs stir and raise themselves once more."

So Nanna went back to Asgard, and shut herself up forlornly in her golden palace till such time as Baldur should bring back her heart.

AN ESTHONIAN FOLK-TALE:
KOIT AND ÄMARIK

Dost thou know the lamp that shines in the All-Father's halls? Just now it is resting; it has gone out. But its reflection still glows through the heavens; and already do the rays of its light turn round towards the East, whence, in its full might, it will ere long salute the whole of Creation.

Dost thou know the hand that receives the sun and leads it to its rest when it has run its course? Or the hand that rekindles it when it has gone out, and sends it forth again on its road through the heavens?

The All-Father had two true servants, whom he endowed with eternal youth. And when the lamp had finished its course the first evening, he said to Ämarik:—

"To thy guard, my daughter, do I commit the sinking sun. Quench it, and have a care with the fire, that no hurt come to pass."

And again, when the time for morning came, he said to Koit:—

"My son, it shall be thy concern to light the lamp and make it ready for a new journey."

Both did their duty faithfully, and on no one day was the lamp wanting from the vault of heaven. And when in winter it wanders along the edge of the sky, then it goes out earlier in the afternoon and sets forth later in the morning. And when in spring it awakens flowers and the songs of birds, and when in summer it ripens the fruit with the heat of its beams, then it has but a short time to rest; Ämarik gives it up at once when it is quenched into the hands of Koit, who breathes a new life into it.

The fair time was now come when the flowers open their perfumed cups, and birds and men fill with songs the hollow of Ilmarinen's tent.[17] Then Koit and Ämarik looked each other too deeply in the eyes, dark as whortle-berries; and when the sun, as it went out, passed from her hand to his, then hand pressed hand, and the lips of the one stirred the lips of the other.

But an eye which ever wakes had marked what was happening in the secrecy of the midnight stillness; and on the morrow the Ancient of Days called them both before him and said:—

"I am fully content with the way in which you fulfil your duties, and I wish you to be completely happy. Marry, then; and wait on your task together as man and wife."

And as with one voice they answered:—"Father, disturb not our gladness. Let us remain ever betrothed groom and bride; for we have found our happiness in this state where loves are ever young and new." And the Ancient of Days granted their request and blessed their resolution.

Once only in the year, during four weeks, do the two meet at midnight. And when Ämarik puts the sun that has gone out into the hand of her lover, there follow a pressure of the hand and a kiss; and Ämarik's cheeks grow red and their rosy hue is reflected through the heavens, until Koit lights the lamp again and the golden sheen in the sky announces the upgoing sun. For that joyous meeting the All-Father adorns his fields with the most lovely flowers; and nightingales cry jestingly to Ämarik as she lingers on Koit's breast: —"Careless girl, careless girl. The night is long."

Translated from the FOSTERLÄNDSKT ALBUM.

TWO TRANSLATIONS FROM THE ITALIAN OF ADA NEGRI

(From "Tempeste," by kind permission of Messrs. Fratelli Treves).

These translations, although they have not received final revision, are included because of the striking character of the originals.

---

[190]
[191]

THE GREAT

WONDER for the Strong! who, forehead-kissed By superhuman lips,

Following the lights of new horizons
   From height of sovereignty,

The smile, the flash, the song of genius
   Had, and its folly;

Knew all its flights and all its tears
   And all its harmonies;

And from their peak launched to the listening world
   Their sacred words;

And died 'mid dreams and symphonies
   Bathed in bright sunlight.

✳   ✳   ✳   ✳   ✳

Love for the Rebels! Heart-bitten, they, By sùpreme anguish;

Linked in Love's leash
   With those who weep, with those who tremble,

With those, outcast, by Christ redeemed,
   By brethren betrayed.

By sea, by land, to thronging crowds
   New laws have they proclaimed;

Have raised the hymn of coming ages,
   Sublimely frenzied

For the ideal; and,—irons, rope or axe—
   Smiled at their torments.

✳   ✳   ✳   ✳   ✳

But for the Great of Gloomy Places,
   Tears, heart-wrung. Such as are

A-hungered, trodden down; and—venerable—
   Nor truce nor pardon knew

From hostile, impious nature,
   Yet hated not.

Who saw the corn-ear spring for others,
   Yet thievèd not.

Whose drink was gall and tears;
   who, traitorously

Lashed in the face by blindfold Tyranny,
   Yet murmured not.

Who walked 'mid frosts and tempests
   Darkling and quite forgot;

No sun, no bread, no clothing,
   Yet trusted God.

Who had a heap of straw to sleep on
   Loathsome and horrible;

A lazar-house to die in,
Yet loving died.

THE WORKMAN

AROUND me rose the city
Stirring at the first glimpse of day;
The great city, that gives bread, that labours,
Rose, as the sun gleamed forth, to its gigantic toil.

There was a crying of clear voices, unknown voices,
Beating waves of sound;
A throwing wide of doors and windows,
A whistling of trains, a whirling of wheels.

There was a hastening gaily, furiously,
Of a thousand human forces
Towards the work that gives health and food,
That unfurls a thousand flags to the wind.

All things glittered, palpitated, laughed
In the glory of the morning;
All things seemed to open wings;
Hope and joy gleamed on every visage.

Then I observed him. Powerful was he: his front—
Pale with thought—
Proudly and nobly bore he
On the bronzed neck, free-moving.

Bull neck—breast of the savage—
Bold glance and word;
In his veins the surge of life,
Billows of love and of bravery.

Resounding the footfall! Like a victor
Advanced he in the light;
And my heart murmured:—Is he not a leader?
Amid the pandemonium

Of the workshop, proud in his workman's blouse,
Does he not tame the monsters
To whom man meted claws and bills,
Soul of flame and thews of steel?

Wells there not within him a fount of vigour,
Leaping, overbearing,
That shall fill with fresh life this languishing age,
Sallow with vice and lack of blood?

Oh blessèd, blessèd to be beloved of him....
To wait for him each evening
Before the frugal board, with all the true
Sweet anxiousness of one who loves and waits.

Blessèd to cull from him, as the white lily
Culls from the golden bee,
The kiss of one who knows grim strife and toil;
To be all his treasure, to bear a son to him:

And in this son, fair and blameless,
Informed with all his father's worth,
To nurse a hope, a hope eternal,

122

To find the joys of a falling world:

And to dream, through him continued
In the centuries to come,
Of the race of the unbowed, of the pure,
Destined to dazzling days of light:

Of an unstained race of slaves redeemed
Who amid songs shall reap
Harvests of freedom born from the weeping,
From the blood, from the very hearts, of their forerunners.

THREE LITERARY STUDIES

GIOSUÉ CARDUCCI

THE Roman historian Niebuhr reviewing the literature of the Augustan age, gave it as his opinion that epic poetry was dead, the lyric form of poetical expression being the only one adapted to the genius of the Romans at that period. Virgil's "Æneid," beautiful as are its details, he considers a failure as an epic; for an epic hero should, with fresh simple spontaneity, go straight home to the heart of the people at large, and this, he argues, the character of Æneas could never have done. Greek legends in Virgil's poem are so dovetailed into the Latin ones that the work loses its national character, loses therefore its spontaneity, and remains now, as it must have been from the beginning, an exquisite mosaic, to be appreciated only by the cultured; and appreciated, moreover, rather for the delicacy of the descriptions and the art of the versification, than for any inherent interest attaching to the principal characters. Roman literary society was, in fact, too positive to produce an epic poem. The sceptical spirit was uppermost. Legend, instead of firing the imagination, did but arouse the critical faculty. The story of Romulus, of his wondrous birth and preservation, of his building of the city, his government, and marvellous death, was neither believed in as fact nor treated as poetry. Men set to work to examine and to explain it; a useful task, no doubt, and one which Niebuhr himself has performed as well as anyone else, but one expressive of a spirit far removed from that which animates the writer of an epic poem. The death of the epic meant, however, the life of the lyric. Occupying themselves but little with the motives and actions of those who lived in other ages, men felt all the more need of uttering their own subjective feelings and impressions. For such utterances they naturally chose the lyric form, which the highly developed æsthetic sense of the time induced them to work to a high degree of perfection. This, in fact, was the age of Horace and Catullus.

Surely much the same causes are at work, in different forms of society, at the present day. The Italian critic Trezza sings the dirge of the epic, and proves that the lyric is the only form of poem possible to the society of the nineteenth century. Another authority besides Trezza makes a similar assertion.

"The epic," he says, "was buried some time ago. To violate the tomb of the mighty dead by singing doggerel over it, even if it were not the sign of a depraved disinclination to undertake higher flights, would not be particularly diverting. The drama (referring to poetic drama) is *in extremis*, and the superabundance of doctors won't even let it depart in peace. Lyric poetry, individual by nature, appears to stand its ground, and may still last some little while provided it does not forget it is an art. If it degrades itself into a mere secretion of the sensibility or sensuality of such and such an one, if it surrenders itself to all the unnatural licences which sensibility and sensuality allow themselves, then, poor lyric, she too is no longer recognisable.... To have adapted to the lyric this style of versification, fit only for narration and description, without verses, and with rhymes *a piacere*, is a sure sign that every idea of the true lyric has been lost.... An asthmatic lyric, paunch-bellied, in dressing-gown of ample girth, and slippers—tie upon it!... I, bending at the foot of the Italian Muse, first kiss it with respectful tenderness, then try to fit on the sapphic, alcaic, and asclepiadaic buskins in which her godlike sister led the choruses on the Parian marble of the Doric temples, which look down at themselves in the sea that was the fatherland of Aphrodite and Apollo."

So writes the great Italian poet Carducci, using a similitude which might have come from the pen of Horace himself. The Augustan age produced a poet who measured the Greek lyric buskins on Latin measures; the nineteenth century has given birth to one who has fitted them on to Italian verse.

Giosué Carducci, whose poetical works have raised so much controversy in Italy, and occasioned a deluge of treatises on metre, Italian and Latin, was born at Valdicastello, in the classic Tuscan land, on July 27th, 1836, of a family which, in the days of the independence of the Tuscan cities, had given a Gonfaloniere to the Florentine Republic. His first impressions of Nature he received from the Pisan Maremma, here stretching away in "peaceful hills, with steaming mists, and green plains smiling in the morning showers"; there in "chalk-hills of malignant aspect, sparsely shaded by wood, with horses wandering under the guilty-looking cork-oaks that bristle, lowering, in the plain below"; or again in "cloud-swept unsown plains, by the widowed shores of the Tuscan sea," scattered with the old-world feudal towers, and full of ancient memories of decayed cities and mediæval strife. It was among such surroundings that at the age of eleven Carducci wrote his first verses. These reveal at once the historical and classical tendency of his mind; for besides a few lines on the "Death of an Owl," we find a poem on "The Fall of the Castle of Bolgheri into the hands of Ladislaus, King of Naples," and another entitled "M. Brutus Meditating the Death of Cæsar."

Those were unsettled times, however. Political revolution deprived Carducci's father in 1849 of his post of village-doctor, and forced him to take refuge in Florence, where Giosué was put to school with the Scolopian Fathers. All readers of Ruffini will remember that author's experience of the Scolopian convent school as described in "Lorenzo Benoni"; and can imagine that Carducci, accustomed to the open life of the Maremma, full of aspirations towards the freedom of classic times, did not feel himself altogether in his element as he sat learning from the black priest whose "clucking voice blasphemed *Io amo*," and "whose face it was vexation to behold."

On leaving school, young Carducci published his first volume of poems; and in 1858, together with some of his friends, started a review named after the famous sixteenth century poet "Il Poliziano." The paper, as is usual with such juvenile ventures, was short-lived; but it is interesting as showing the efforts the young poet was already making towards the adaptation of classical forms to modern ideas. It was, however, impossible that any ardent youth should content himself with mere literary form during that period of ferment which resulted in the formation of a United Italy. He, like his contemporaries throughout the length and breadth of the land, was fired by the noble efforts made by Garibaldi and Mazzini for the redemption of their fatherland from the hated Austrian yoke; and, though republican by tradition (as all Italians must be) as well as by natural inclination, Carducci was yet willing to follow the moderate party and Garibaldi in their support of the monarchy of Savoy. Speaking of his political views at that time, he says:—

"I was one of the very many who in '59 and '60 adopted the formula of the Garibaldini, 'Italy and Victor Emmanuel,' without any enthusiasm for the moderate party and its leaders, but loyally. I was drawn to it partly from grateful affection for the King and Piedmont, in whose firmness I had found some consolation for the misery of the preceding ten years; partly from the idea that in the fusion of the noble with the burgher element, of the army with the people, of the monarchical traditions of one part of the country with the democratic traditions of other parts, in the intimate union of loyalty with liberty, of discipline with enthusiasm, of ancient tradition with modern belief, the history of Italy—that history of wondrous tissue, which bears within itself all the seeds, developments, blossomings, fadings of all political ideas, forms and phenomena—will at length find, better than the Greek could have done, its necessary unfolding and complement, achieving the liberation, the union, the greatness of the whole country by means of the valour and strength of the nation, without, and even in opposition to, any foreign interference."

As this extract clearly shows, Carducci's attachment to the Moderates (as he calls the Monarchists) was purely Platonic; his natural passion was for the Republicans. Such dualism between head and heart, such war between his just idea of the exigencies of modern times and his fervid admiration of the methods and life of the classic world, soon brought him into serious difficulties, and rendered his active participation in the military and political events of the Sixties null. For the men with whom he found himself associated as colleagues, though at one with him as regards the fundamental tenet of the necessity of a monarchy, had but little understanding of his idea that the valour and strength of the nation was to be the making of Italy, without foreign interference, or even in opposition to it. They relied more on modern methods of diplomacy than on Greek dash and daring; and, to gain their ends, were ready to compromise with other Powers and with the Church in a way that clashed with Carducci's classic enthusiasm. Hence the poet was forced into opposition to the party to which his reflection politically attached him, and poured out the bitterness of his soul for the indignities inflicted on his ideal, in a series of poems afterwards collected and published in a little volume bearing the title of "Giambi ed Epodi" ("Iambics and Epodes"). This attitude naturally led the Moderate party into the belief that Carducci was a preacher of republicanism. As such they persecuted him, even suspending him from his chair of Italian Literature at Bologna; and as such he has ever been considered until he fell under the spell of the extraordinary fascination exerted by the grace and manners of Queen Margherita. Under this spell his old admiration for the House of Savoy revived, becoming, as many think, exaggerated. He was reproached as a turncoat by those who never fully understood his former opinions or his true attitude with regard to the Moderate party; he lost caste among the students, who once kept him for a whole hour in his lecture-room while they hissed him violently; and the people at large, finding him turned into a court poet, openly asserted that he was in his decadence, and that his latter end was not worthy his beginning. It is certainly a pity for his fame that it should have been, of all persons, the Queen in whom he found so warm and appreciative a friend; for his constant presence about her in the summer holidays doubtless laid him open, for many minds, to the charge of snobbism. Two things, however, must be remembered in his defence. Firstly, that he has always considered monarchy as necessary for Italy in her present condition; secondly, that the combination of military glory with grace and culture has been his ideal from boyhood; and this combination he found represented in King Umberto and Queen Margherita. One of his later poems, "War" ("La Guerra") which hymns the praises of military enterprise, clearly shows that he has lost nothing of his ancient admiration for martial prowess; while others, addressed to Queen Margherita, prove also his poetic sensibility to feminine grace. It is thus easy to explain Carducci's apparent change of attitude, while at the same time fully understanding that the masses—not apt to enquire into the workings of a man's mind, not apt to read with much attention or reflection—are simply struck by the difference in tone between his earlier poems (the "Ça Ira" in honour of the French Revolution, for instance), and his later laudations of the House of Savoy, and launch against him the charge to which we have alluded.

It is difficult to choose, from the scathing scorn of the "Giambi" ("Iambics"), poured out in the incisive terseness of Carducci's verse, any short passage which should give an idea of the whole series. We may mention, however, the terrible little poem entitled "Meminisse Horret," written in 1867 while the Court was at Florence. He describes a horrible nightmare in which he sees Italy giving the lie to all her past traditions. Her ancient heroes are turned into cowards and supplicate those whom once they proudly defied; Dante, dressed like a clown, obsequiously shows strangers round Santa Croce; while Machiavelli, peeping slyly from behind a tomb, proclaims with a wink the adulteries of his mother-country in few words which cut to the quick. In the poem, written on the death of Giovanni Cairoli, the youth who, like his three brothers before him, died in battle for the unity of his country, to the grief yet glory of his widowed mother, the poet, branding, as Dante might have done, the infamy of those who dance and make love, and bring Italy to shame on the very graves of her heroes, goes so far as to curse his fatherland:—

> ...   . Cursed
> be thou, my ancient fatherland,
> on whom to-day's shame and the vengeance
> of the centuries lie heaped!
>
> The plant of valour grows here yet
>   but for thy mules
>
> to bed on; here the violet's perfume
> ends in the dung-heap.

Bitter, too, are the verses entitled "Italy's Song as she goes up the Campidoglio." The mode, namely, in which the Italian Government, after promising in the September Convention that it would not occupy Rome, slunk into the city while France and Germany were busy with their own affairs, revolted Carducci's whole soul, much as he, like all true Italian patriots, desired to set the Capitol as crown and seal on United Italy. He represents the army as entering stealthily by night, and calling on the Capitoline geese not to make such a dreadful clatter; it's only "Italy, great and united," who is coming back to her own again, and they'll wake Cardinal Antonelli if they cackle so. We might quote endlessly to show how intensely despicable Carducci considered the diplomats of the Moderate party, who tried to gain their ends by crooked negotiations now with one Power, now with another, boasting that they had "read their Machiavelli"; and its generals who led out the fiery Italian youth to be slaughtered by the enemy. Nothing can equal, however, the concentration of scorn to be found in the sonnet "Heu Pudor":—

> He lies who says that, when the heart flares up,
> the breath of heated genius fans it.
> With the eternal stamp of infamy had I too
> branded the front of this unworthy herd.
>
> As fierce mayhap as thine, oh Dante father,
> the hate and scorn that camp within my heart;
> But their voracious flaming roars enclosed,
> destroying me, and ne'er attains its aim.
>
> New lakes of pitch, made thick
> with serpents, monsters, and with demons harsh
> a new and twofold bolgia had I dug;
> and, with its hills and with its walls, cast in—
> like to a loathsome tatter—
> this fatherland of Fucci and Bonturi.[18]

It must not be thought, however, that Carducci can emit nothing but fire and smoke. From the lurid "Giambi" we can turn for relief to the exquisite little word-pictures of the "Odi Barbare" and of many of the poems published in the collections entitled "Levia Gravia" and "Rime Nuove." It is in these that Carducci's sense of nature, frank classic paganism, united curiously, however, to a certain German sentimental pessimism, and his extraordinary power of word-sculpture reveal themselves.

Let no reader of Burns or Hogg expect to find in Carducci, however, the same type of nature-sense as abounds in the Saxon poets. The clear sky and sharp outlines of Italy do not encourage that gentle sentiment produced by the misty vagueness of hills and plains in the rain-laden atmosphere of the north. A poet of Greek-Latin race is not likely to give us the "Address to a Mountain Daisy," the sweet tenderness of "Kilmeny," the undefined melancholy of Tennyson's "Dying Swan," or even the cradling lusciousness of "Haroun Al-Raschid." His landscape is altogether larger; his sky, clear, "stripped to its depths," as Shelley says of that of Venice, renders distinct even small distant details of scarped or forest-clad hill, and, reflected in lake or sea or lighting up the mountains with amethyst and topaz, gives colours of greater brilliancy, though of less mystic warmth and depth, than does the ever-varying atmosphere of the British Isles. Macaulay and Longfellow have already observed the difference of the two types of mind in the exactitude of detail to be observed in Dante's "Inferno" as compared with the vagueness of Milton's "Hell," and it is very noticeable also in the nature-descriptions of lyric poets. Take as an instance the opening of the following poem "All'Aurora" "To the Dawn":—

"Thou risest and kissest the clouds with thy rosy breath, O Goddess,

Kissest the darkling tops of marble temples.

The woods feel thee and rouse with a chilly shudder,

The falcon springs upon the wing with robber joy,

Whilst the garrulous nests are full of whisperings among the damp leaves,

And the sea-gull screams grey over the purple sea.

In the laborious plain the first to rejoice in thee are the rivers,

Glittering tremulously among the murmurs of the poplars:

The sorrel foal runs joyfully towards the deep-flowing streams,

His maned head erect, neighing to the winds:

The watchful valour of the dogs gives answer from the cabins

And the whole valley resounds with lusty lowings.

But man, whom thou awakenest to consume his life in work,

Still regards thee with thoughtful admiration,

Just as, in time gone by, the noble Aryan fathers

Upright among their white flocks adored thee on the mountain."

It is a pity that it is impossible for us to give the subtle melody of Carducci's verse. Although French and German poets have recognised the master and translated some of his works, no Englishman appears to have as yet shown this mark of appreciation. Nevertheless, the characteristic way of treating the subject is clearly visible. The hawk, emblem of freedom and strife, is the first living creature that strikes the poet's eye and mind. The sea-gull, the galloping foal, then the baying of the dogs and the "lusty lowings," render an impression rather of grandeur than tenderness; the smaller birds are hardly mentioned, the landscape is clear and exact. At the same time there are little touches of exquisite beauty, worthy of Virgil himself, as in the "rosy breath" with which the Dawn kisses the clouds, the "chilly shudder of the woods," "the garrulous nests whispering among the damp leaves." Such jewels of expression are indeed scattered throughout the whole of Carducci's work, their conciseness rendering very apparent the classicality of the models on which Carducci formed his style. Of him, indeed, Tennyson might have said, as he did of Virgil—

> "All the wealth of all the Muses,
> often flowering in a lonely word."

Spring sets Carducci's heart beating in dithyrambs; it is in his spring songs that he abandons himself most completely to the joy of life as life, and attains, perhaps, some of his highest flights of lyric song. Very beautiful, for instance, are the three poems entitled "Greek Spring Songs": i. Æolic; ii. Doric; iii. Alexandrine. From the first of these we may quote the return of Apollo

> "from the hyperborean shores to the pious soil of Greece, to the laurels from the sluggish cold; two white swans draw him as they fly: the sky smiles. On his head he bears Jove's golden fillet, but the air sighs in his thick-growing locks, and the lyre moves in his hand with amorous trembling. Around him circle in light dance the Cyclades, fatherland of the deity; from afar Cyprus and Cythera send up white foam of applause. And a slight skiff follows throughout the great Ægean, purple-sailed, harmonious: Alcæus of the golden plectrum, bearing arms, guides it through the waters. Sappho sits in the midst of it, with soft smile and hyacinthine tresses, her white breast heaving in the ambrosial air which streams from the god."

The poet is not always so classical as this, however. Of a very different stamp, to select one other out of many spring poems, is his "Brindisi d'Aprile" ("April Drinking Song")—

> "When, in the dark ilexes and new-flowered almond, revels the nuptial chorus of the birds, and the primroses on the sunny hills are eyes of old-world nymphs looking out on mortal men, and the sun greets the beds of flowers with youthful smile, and over the silent moor the sky bends piously, and the breath of April moves the flowering corn like a sigh of love stirring a young bride's veil; then do the trunk of the vine and the heart of the maiden leap up with throbs; they feel their wounds. The vine breathes odorous buds into the cold twigs, the maiden darts desire in her virgin blushes. Everything ferments and grows languid in the tepor of the air: the blood within the veins, the wine within the casks. O, ruddy prisoner! thou yearnest for thy fatherland, and the breath of thy native hill raises a ferment within the tun. There is the joyous life of the vine twigs: here thou art a prisoner in the snare.... Hurrah for liberty! Let us go, let us go to liberate the captive; let us call him back to life and make him sparkle in the glass, sparkle on the crest of the hill, sparkle to the sunlight; let the light breeze kiss him again; let him behold the young vines."

And yet with all this revelling in nature, and especially the nature of spring-time, the melancholy despondent strain is never far distant. Even in the

Greek spring songs there is nearly as much talk of chill mist and rain as of clear sky and sunlight; and the third song, the Alexandrine, goes so far as to even introduce a graveyard. In the little poem entitled "School Memories," too, the poet, after describing the priest, makes a charming picture of the summer landscape and beckoning trees that he sees through the window: but everything is suddenly crossed and darkened by the thought of "death, and the formless nothing," and this thought of death has haunted him ever since. He is too fond of graveyards; too apt, like some German poets at the beginning of last century, to look upon the world as a vast cemetery. It is perhaps to this same strain of pessimism, this same tendency to look at the ugly side of things, that we are to attribute the absolute repulsiveness of many of the images he employs. To compare trees, bald, dripping, and bent, to sextons over a grave is hardly poetical, but it is at any rate harmless; some of his other similitudes are too repulsive for translation, and we must think it a pity that so great a poet should encourage the tendency to dwell, quite gratuitously, on disagreeable non-poetical subjects.

Perhaps the poems which are most free from these defects are those contained in the first volume of the "Odi Barbare." There we find the exquisite little piece entitled "Fantasia."

> "Thou speakest and thy voice's soul, yielding languidly to the gentle breeze, floats out over the caressing waves, and sails to strange shores. It sails smiling in a tepor of setting sunlight, into the solitudes: white birds fly between sky and sea, green islands pass by, the temples on their rocky summits dart rays of Parian whiteness in the rosy sunset, the cypresses on the shores tremble, and the thick myrtles send forth their odour. The smell of the salt breezes wanders afar, and mingles with the slow singing of the sailors, whilst a ship within sight of the harbour peacefully furls its red sails. Maidens come down from the acropolis in long procession, and they have beautiful white peplums, they bear garlands on their heads, in their hands they have branches of laurel, they extend their arms and sing. His spear planted in the sand of his fatherland, a man leaps to earth, glittering in arms: is he perchance Alcæus come back from war to the Lesbian virgins."

To see the charming way in which Carducci can blend history with nature, we must turn in the same volume to the poem entitled "Sull' Adda."

> "Flow through the red fires of evening, flow, blue Adda: Lydia on the placid stream, with tender love, sails towards the setting sun. Behold, the memorable bridge fades behind us: the airy spring of the arches yields to the distance and sinks to the level of the liquid plain that widens and murmurs."

And then the poet, in musical verse, traces the history of the battles between the Romans and barbarians; speaks of the "pale Corsican who passed the dubious bridge amid lightnings, bearing the fate of two centuries in his slight and youthful hand"; and in contrast with the smoke and clang and blood of battle we have the recurrence of the verse representing Lydia floating through the fires of evening towards the setting sun: "Beneath the Olympic smile of the air the earth palpitates: every wave glows and rises trembling, swelling with radiant love." The smell of youthful meadows rises from either bank, the great trees sign to the skiff as it passes, and, descending from the trees and rising from the flowering hedges, the birds follow through the gold and rosy streaks (of sky and water), mingling joyful loves. Between rich meadows the Adda flows on to lose itself in the Eridano; the untiring sun sinks to its setting.

> "O sun, O flowing Adda!" exclaims the poet, "the soul floats through an elysium behind thee; where will it and mutual love lose themselves, O Lydia? I know not; but I would lose myself now far from men, in Lydia's languid glance, where float unknown desires and mysteries."

His power of blending historical scenes with descriptive poetry is also to be found in the poem entitled "At the Springs of the Clitunnus." Umbrians, Tuscans, Romans, Carthaginians pass before the reader; then Catholicism appears with its black-robed priests, driving out ancient gods and tillage, but ousted in its turn by new developments of the human mind. "Before us the train, steaming and panting after new industries, whistles as it rushes along." Strange as it may seem, all this history does not swamp the poetry, which is of the most purely idyllic character throughout.

We must not leave the subject of Carducci's sympathy with nature without mentioning the pretty little dialogue between the poet and the great alley of cypress-trees at which he used to fling stones, and among which he used to go bird-nesting in his boyish days. The cypresses run to meet him like a double row of young giants, welcome him and beg him to remain with them, offering him the pastimes of years gone by. The poet answers that he cannot stop; he has grown to be a celebrity now, he reads Greek and Latin, writes and writes, is no longer an urchin, and, as to stones, he no longer throws them, especially at plants. A murmur runs through the doubting summits, the rosy light of the setting sun shines athwart the dark cypress green with a pitying smile, sun and trees seem to feel compassion for him, and the murmur embodies itself in words. The winds have told the poet's old companions of his eternal unrest, of his eternal brooding over vexed questions which can never be settled. Let him come back to his old haunts, to the blue sea, the smile of the setting sun, the flights of birds, the chirping of the sparrows, the choruses which pass eternally between earth and sky. So only will he lay the evil spectres which rise from the black depths of man's thought-beaten heart, as putrid flames rise before one walking in a cemetery. The poet will not stop, yet, as the train whirls him back to the problems of the world, he looks back at the quiet graveyard to which they lead up and where his grandmother lies, wondering whether they may not be right, and whether what he has sought for morning and evening so many years in vain, may not after all be hidden there. Yet as the train rushes on, the colts run racing beside it; and it is only a donkey, feeding on a thistle, that stands stolidly gazing on the busy scene before him.

A pilgrim to this cypress alley relates that its owner, Count Walfredo della Gherardesca, refuses to cut down the trees, many of which have suffered much from storms, and replant the alley. "Carducci loves them," he said, "and therefore I respect them. Those that have suffered I shall replace little by little by young plants, and thus the alley will preserve its true and now celebrated appearance."

As an expression of pure nature-sense, we may still quote, perhaps, the sonnet entitled "The Ox":—

> "I love thee, O pious ox; a gentle sentiment of strength and peace dost thou infuse into my heart, whether, solemn, monumental, thou lookest out over the free and fertile fields, or whether, bending to the yoke, thou secondest man's swift work with grave content: he urges thee, he goads thee, and thou answerest with the slow turn of thy patient eyes. Thy breath streams from thy nostril large and damp and black, and thy lowing loses itself in the still air like a joyous hymn; and within the grave sweetness of thine eye, with its green-shadowed depths, the divine verdure of the plain lies reflected broadly and tranquilly."

The conciseness and precision of Carducci's language give him an extraordinary power of vivid representation of his subject. He "etches, sculptor-like," as Emerson says of Dante. What can be more vivid, for instance, than the picture of rural life which opens the poem "At the Springs of the Clitunnus"?—

> "Still do the flocks come down to thee, O Clitunnus, through the moist air of evening, from the mountain that waves with dusky ash-groves murmuring in the wind, and scatters afar its odours of wild sage and thyme; the Umbrian boy still plunges the struggling sheep into thy wave; whilst the babe at the breast of the sunburnt mother, sitting barefoot by the cottage door and singing, turns towards him, and smiles from its fair round face; thoughtfully does the father, his legs clad in goat-skins like the fauns of old, guide the painted ploughshare, and the strength of the beautiful heifers; the beautiful square-breasted heifers their heads erect with mooned horns, sweet-eyed, snowy, that gentle Virgil loved."

Does not one see before one, too, the *Bionda Maria* (fair-haired Maria) of the "Idillio Maremmano" in the following verses?

> "How lovely wert thou, O maiden, emerging from the long waving furrows, with fresh-plucked flowers in thy hand, tall and smiling; and under thy glowing brows thou opened'st the blue of thy large deep eyes darting untamed fire. Like the cornflower among the yellowing gold of the corn-ears did the blue of that eye blossom forth among thy tawny hair; and before and around thee the height of summer flamed; the sun laughed, broken by the green branches of the pomegranate, sparkling in red. At thy passing, as at that of a goddess, the gorgeous peacock opened his eyed tail, beholding thee, and sent up to thee a harsh cry."

Of a different kind, but equally effective, is the following description, drawn from a scene in the hall of a thirteenth-century lord. The storm is raging outside; the greyhound bays at the thunder, and stretches out his taper head, with erect ears and restless eyes, towards the marchioness who sits amid her women and maidens; a fire, smelling of the pine forest, blazes in the midst, and, upright before it, Malaspina rises a whole head above the minor barons:—

> "A fine trained goshawk perched on the knight's fist, and, when the hail struck the windows now here now there according to the shifting wind, and the swift-passing lightning

whitened the flashing arms hanging on the walls, the bird beat its wings, stretching out its snakelike neck, and gave out a hoarse cry of joy: the love of his native, free Apuan heights burnt in his piercing eye; he longed, the noble bird, to direct his flight through the thunder athwart the clouds."

Diverse once more, yet none the less apt to remain impressed upon the memory, is the opening picture of the poem for the fifth anniversary of the battle of Mentana, where, it will be remembered, Garibaldi's troops were defeated by the combined French and Papal forces:—

"Every year when the sad hour of Mentana's rout sounds over the conscious hills, plains and hills heave, and proudly upright stands the band of the dead on the tumuli of Nomentum. They are no hideous skeletons; they are tall and beautiful forms, around which waves the rosy veil of twilight: through their wounds laugh the pious, virgin stars; the clouds of the sky wreathe lightly round their locks."

No doubt it is Carducci's classicism (in a poem entitled "Classicism and Romanticism" he holds up the latter to utter ridicule) which gives him this marked power of word-painting; it also informs his poem with a paganism of which we shall have presently to speak. Yet it is classicism deeply coloured by nineteenth-century life. Take, for instance, the little poem "Ruit Hora," and see how the modern unrest comes across the calm of the classic scene. Horace's Lydia would not have understood a lover of this sort for all his passion:—

"O green solitude for which I have yearned, far from the noise of men! hither come two divine friends with us, O Lydia, Wine and Love. See how Lycæus, the eternal youth, laughs in the shining crystal: as in thine eyes, O glorious Lydia, Love rides in triumph and unbinds his eyes. The sun shines low through the trellis and breaks, rosy, against my glass; he glances and trembles golden among thy locks, O Lydia. Among the blackness of thy locks, O snowy Lydia, a pallid rose languishes, and a gentle sudden sadness tempers the fires of love in my heart. Tell me: why does the sea down there send up mysterious groanings under the flaming evening? What songs, O Lydia, do those pines sing to each other? See with what desire those hills stretch out their arms to the setting sun: the shadow grows and embraces them: it seems as though they were begging the last kiss, O Lydia. I beg thy kisses, if the shade envelops me, O Lycæus, giver of joy; I beg thine eyes, O shining Lydia, if Hyperion sinks. And time is rushing by. O rosy mouth, unclose! O flower of the soul, O flower of desire, open thy cup! O loved arms, open!"

Perhaps, too, Carducci, for all his classic forms, is the only living poet who could make a detailed description of a railway station, the arrival of the train, clipping of the ticket, banging of the doors, etc., without once falling into triviality or bombast; yet such a feat has he performed in the poem entitled, "At the Station on an Autumn Morning."

Especially marked in Carducci's poems, and particularly in his early ones, is his rebellion against the Church. The poet's paganism has been much discussed. It is a paganism based not on any repugnance for the teaching and character of Christ (on the contrary, the poet makes a most attractive picture of Christ in one of his poems), but upon the unfeigned joy in nature with which, as an antidote to his own pessimism, the classic poets presented him. It takes the form of a violent revolt against the creed that, in his opinion, had neglected if not opposed art, had raved of "atrocious unions of God with Pain," had substituted gloom and sadness for the happy life of freedom and nature (see the poem entitled "In a Gothic Church"), had for centuries been a barrier to human progress, had constantly been found in alliance with the enemies of Italy, and had, in these later years of ardent strife for the unification of the Fatherland, systematically, with violence and with cunning, opposed the heroes who were giving their lives in the cause of freedom. The Romish Church was for him the symbol of retrogression, gloom, and antipatriotism; and in the violence of his reaction against it he confounded it with the whole of Christianity, even going so far as to personify progress and liberty, by antithesis, under the title of "Satan."

The "Hymn to Satan," published for the first time in 1865 at Pistoia under the pseudonym of "Enotrio Romano," may be said, indeed, to be the beginning of his fame. Launched on the world without any explanation, the misleading title caused it to be understood only by a few careful readers. The world at large saw in it, according to the opinion of one critic, "an intellectual orgy," a blasphemous rebellion against everything that the nation, and even the world, had hitherto considered sacred and necessary for the existence of society. Its publication excited great controversy, afterwards given to the world under the title of the "Polemiche Sataniche," which gave Carducci the opportunity of responding to the attacks of the critics, and explaining the intimate sense of the poem; but even after his explanations, even when we know from his own lips that for him, taking up, as he believes, the standpoint of the modern Roman Catholic Church, "Satan is beauty, love, wellbeing, happiness"; that "Satan is thought that flies, science that experiments, the heart that blazes up, the forehead on which is written 'I will not abase myself'; that Satanic were the revolutions that brought men out of the middle ages; Satanic the Italian communes; the German Reformation; Holland embodying liberty in deed; England vindicating and avenging it; France spreading it abroad to all orders and all peoples,"—even after the poet himself has told us this, the poem still jars in many places for the unwonted violence of its expressions. It is a battle-hymn, with all the fire and energy of the battle-charge in it. The metre rushes like the swift running of horses, sweeping the reader along with irresistible force. The poem opens with the following invocation:—

"Towards thee, boundless principle of being, matter and spirit, reason and sense, whilst the wine sparkles in the cups like the soul in the eye; while the earth and sun smile and interchange words of love, and a murmur of mysterious nuptials runs through the mountains, and the fruitful plain palpitates,—towards thee does the bold verse break forth; I invoke thee, O Satan, king of the feast. Away, O priest, with your aspersorium and your chant! No, priest, Satan turns not back. See, rust eats away Michael's mystic brand; and the faithful archangel, plucked of his feathers, falls into space. Cold is the thunderbolt in Jehovah's hand. Like pallid meteors, extinguished planets, do the angels rain down from the firmaments. In never-sleeping matter, king of phenomena, king of forms, Satan lives alone."

Satan lurks in beauty, love, and wine, so the poem goes on; and Satan breathes "from my verse if, bursting forth from my breast and defying the god of guilty priests, of bloody kings, it shakes the minds of men like a thunderbolt." It was Satan who breathed in the nature-worship of ancient times; Satan that, driven out by the barbarous Nazarene fury of the love-feasts whose sacred torches were used to burn down temples, took refuge among the hearth-gods of the people, and shook the breasts of witches, who, pale with eternal care, drew their inspiration from nature and him. He opens the cloister gate before the alchemist, revealing new and radiant skies. In vain monks and nuns try to shut him out from their lives; he inspires Heloïse, he murmurs the verses of Ovid and Horace among David's psalms and tears of repentance. But Satan often peoples the sleepless cell with images of a better age. He arouses, from the pages of Livy, eager tribunes, consuls, agitated shouting crowds. Wiclif and Huss, Savonarola, Luther secure the triumph of human thought: matter, rise again! Satan has conquered.

> "A beautiful and terrible monster breaks loose, traverses the ocean, traverses the land: shining and smoke-wreathed like the volcano, it climbs mountains, devours plains, leaps gulfs; then hides in nameless caves traversing deep-hidden paths; and issues forth; and untamed sends out its cry like a whirlwind from shore to shore, like a whirlwind scatters abroad its breath: he passes, O peoples, Satan the Great,—passes beneficent from place to place on the resistless chariot of fire. Hail, O Satan, O rebellion, O avenging force of reason! Sacred are the vows and the incense that rise to thee. Thou hast conquered the Jehovah of the priest."

The metre of the "Inno a Satana" is, as we have said, swinging and free. It is not in this poem that Carducci has "measured the lyric buskins on to Italian Muse"; and indeed he himself, in the "Polemiche Sataniche," severely criticises its form. It was the expression of the poet's inmost soul, written at white-heat in a single night. Carducci's real work as a lyric poet is to be found in his other poems, in the three volumes of "Odi Barbare," for instance, the "Levia Gravia," the "Rime Nuove," the "Giambi ed Epodi."

> "I have called these odes barbarous," he tells us, "because they would sound so in the ears and judgment of the Greeks and Romans, although I have attempted to compose them in the metrical form of their lyric poetry. I felt," he goes on to say in substance, "that I had different things to say from those sung by Dante, Petrarch, Politian, Tasso, and other classic lyric poets, and could not see why, since Horace and Catullus were allowed to enrich Latin verse with Greek forms, since Dante might adapt Provençal rhymes to Italian poetry, why I should not be pardoned for doing that for which those great poets received praise."

Neither is Carducci alone in his attempts to adapt Latin measures to Italian verse. Other poets (among them Chiabrera) had written *Poesia Barbara* before him, and his contemporary Cavallotti has tried it too; but they have produced *Poesia Barbara* of a different kind. The essential difference between these poets and Carducci lies in this: that whereas they copied the mechanism of the Latin metre, with its complicated system of long and short syllables, Carducci, with finer intuition of the genius of his mother-tongue, has aimed at catching and reproducing the music, the rhythm of the Latin verse. He is hence no copyist but a musician of most delicate ear, whose keen sense of harmony has procured him success where others have failed, and are likely to fail miserably. Modern Italian is not fitted, any more than modern English, for the formal construction of verse on the basis of long and short feet,—on the basis, that is, of metre. Indeed many Italian critics think that even in Latin this form of verse-construction was gradually giving way, or assimilating itself to the rhythmical verse—the verse whose movement struck the ear, as does the rhythm of music or dance, without awakening grammatical considerations of length or shortness of syllables. It is this reproduction of rhythm instead of metre that renders Carducci so eminently and pleasurably readable where other poets, even great ones, are insupportable. All readers of Tennyson, for instance, know the rage with which one tries to infuse a little music into his "experiments." One struggles with "Boadicea," trying vainly to discover some sort of melody in it, but, on coming to such a line as this—

"Mad and maddening, all that heard her in her fierce volubility,"

really throws away the book in utter despair. Not so with Carducci. It is rare to find a harsh verse in his work, though such, of course, do occur here and there, and the ease with which his poetry can be translated into Latin (as much of it has been) proves its close affinity with this language.[19]

As will be seen from the foregoing sketch, Carducci is no easy-going poet. He bears out in his everyday work the dislike he has expressed at seeing the Lyric in dressing-gown and slippers, and has given us, in a little poem at the end of the "Rime Nuove," his idea of what a poet should be—the true *poietes* (ποιητής) of the Greeks. For him the poet is a great artificer, with muscles hardened into iron at his trade: he holds his head high, his neck is strong, his breast bare, his eye bright. Hardly do the birds begin to chirp, and the dawn to smile over the hills than he, with his bellows, rouses the joy of the leaping flames in his smithy. Into the blazing furnace he throws the elements of love and thought, and the memories and glory of his fathers and his people. Past and future does he fuse in the incandescent mass. Then with his hammer he works it on the anvil, and in the splendour of the newly risen sun, sings as he fashions swords to strive for liberty, wreaths to crown victory and glory, and diadems to deck out beauty. "And for himself the poor workman makes a golden arrow, which he shoots towards the sun: his eye follows its shining upward flight, follows it and rejoices, and desires nothing more."

GIOVANNI PASCOLI

THOROUGHLY Italian and of the best period is Pascoli in the exquisite propriety of his words; in the sharpness with which he outlines the little pictures, which are characteristic, especially, of his earlier work. In these respects one feels his close affinity with the Latin poets—above all Virgil—who are his Gods, and from whom the early Italian poets immediately derive. Less Italian— using the word in the stereotyped sense which would exclude Leopardi altogether from Italian song—less Italian is he in the mode and direction of his thought. No gay love-songs, no easy sentimentality have come from his pen: the passion of love is in fact strangely absent from his work. He is a child not so much of Italy, as of his age, in his attitude of enquiry towards the great questions of life and death; in the gravity, the earnestness resulting, especially in his later works, from this attitude.

Nor is this individuality to be wondered at; for Pascoli's muse was cradled in sorrow. He was but a lad when his father, returning home, among the hills of Romagna and within sight of the mediæval republic of S. Marino, was treacherously murdered by an unknown hand. His mother died not very long after, having never really recovered from the shock; then three brothers and a sister; so that Giovanni found himself at a very early age head of a family of a brother and two sisters.

A hard struggle enabled him to form a home for them. One of the little poems to his mother which mark, year after year, the anniversary of her death, refers to this struggle as follows:—

> Know—and perhaps thou dost know in the churchyard—
>   the child with long gold ringlets
>   and that other for whom thy last tear fell—
>   know that I fostered them, that I adore them.
>
> For them I gathered up my shattered courage
>   and I wiped clear my soul for them;
>   they have a roof, they have a nest—my boast:
>   my love it is that feeds them, and my toil.
>
> They are not happy, know it, but serene;
>   theirs is the smile but of a pious sadness:
>   I look on them—my sole, lone family—
>
> and ever to my eyes I feel there comes
>   that last unfinished tear that wet thy lids
>   in the death-agony.

He now lives either at Messina, where he is Professor of Latin, or among the chestnut woods that clothe the hills round Barga near Lucca, with one of his sisters. This is Maria, the careful, winning housewife whom all readers of her brother's poems love—herself known also in the world of letters as a graceful poetess and an accomplished Latin scholar. Two or three verses of the little poem entitled "*Sorella*" reflect the bond that unites them.

> I know not if she be to him more mother
> or more daughter, the sister, gently serious;
> she—sweet, and grave and pious—
> corrects, consoles and counsels;
>
> Presses his hair, embraces him
> care-burdened; speaks:—"*What is it?*"
> Conceals her face against his breast,
> Speaks, in confusion:—"*Know 'st not?*"
>
> She keeps on her pale face
> and in her eyes quick glancing,
> ah! for when he leaves, the smile;
> the tears for his return.

Two principal influences, then, have gone to the moulding of Pascoli's genius: one, the potent attraction of the Augustan poets; the other, the shock, strain and struggle which have fixed his thoughts on the most painful problems of existence; which have, by the very breaking up of his home, accentuated the longing for the domestic affections above that for amorous passion; and have tinged the whole of his work with an autumn-like sadness.

Both these influences reveal themselves in Pascoli's first published work; a small volume of little poems entitled *Myricæ*, and bearing the legend *Arbusta juvant, humilesque myricæ*. The shock was at that time, however, still too near to have exerted its full influence on the poet's character. It kept his mind fixed not so much on the philosophical as on the sentimental and physical side of death: on the churchyard with its cypresses, its driving showers and gleams of golden sunshine, its rainbow, its groups of merry children playing "Touch" round the great cross—but, also, with its dead lying through the long nights of rain and wind. Even here, however, where triteness would seem inevitable, Pascoli is individual. He never contemplates physical decay: worms and skulls are not so much as hinted at. It is the loneliness of his dead that rivets the poet's thoughts, their vain longing for news of those they left on earth:—

> Oh, children—groans the father 'mid the black
> swish of the water—ye whom I hear no more
> for many years! Another churchyard
>
> perhaps received you, and maybe you call
> your mother as you shiver naked
> 'neath the black hissing rainstorms.
>
> And from your far-off dwelling you stretch out
> your arms to me, as I do mine to you,
> oh sons, in vain despair.
>
> Oh, children, children! Could I only see you!

For I would tell you how in that one instant
for an entire eternity I loved you.

In that one minute ere I died
I raised my hand up to my bleeding head,
and blessed you all, my children.

And again:—

They weep. I see, see, see. They form
a circle, wrapped in the ceaseless booming.
They still wait, and they must wait.

The dead sons cling about the father
unavenged. Sits in a tomb,
I see, I see in midst of them, my mother.

Sunt lacrymae rerum. Pascoli returns to his father's death more than once
in these early poems: never with impotent cries against man or destiny, but
with a sense as it were of wide-eyed wonder at the pity of the thing. Here are
a few verses characteristic of his attitude; characteristic, too, of his daring
simplicity of expression, relieved, just as there is a fear of its sinking into
mere prose, by some equally daring conception that throws a vivid light over
all that has gone before.

August 10th.

St. Laurence' day. I know't, because so many
stars through the quiet air
burn, fall; because so great a weeping
gleams in the concave sky.

A swallow was returning to her roof;
they killed her; 'mid the thorns she fell
She had an insect in her beak:
the supper for her nestlings.

Now she lies there as on a cross, and holds
that worm out to that far-off sky;
and in the shadow waits for her her nest;
its chirping fainter comes and fainter.

A man, too, was returning to his nest.
They killed him; he spoke: Pardon!
And in his open eyes remained a cry.
He bore two dolls as gifts....

There in the lonely cottage, now,
in vain they wait and wait for him:
He motionless, astonished, shows
the dolls to the far-off sky.

And thou, oh sky, from far above the worlds
serene—infinite sky, immortal—
oh! with thick-falling tears of stars inundate
this atom dark of Evil.

Such poems bear, however, but a small proportion to the rest of the work
even in the first edition of the *Myricæ*, and a still smaller proportion in the
later editions. The note is struck and left for a time: heard again, it has been
developed into a theme whose harmonies are rich and deep.

The *Myricæ*, now in its fifth edition, is a collection of the shortest of poems. Many of them are but a few lines long, that pass in Italian like the brush of wings and cannot be rendered in our heavier English. Now it is a little picture, cut like a sixteenth century cameo, of some detail of the country or of country life, generally with just a touch at the end that relieves the feeling of pure objectiveness, and suggests the Infinite which lies around and behind the fragment presented; now it is some philosophical maxim or reflection which has evidently become part of the poet's individuality; now an impression of infancy, childhood, girlhood, old age; now a fine-wrought point of irony to prick the ignorance and arrogance of the Philistine.

A consideration of Pascoli's relation to Nature and the peasantry immediately suggests a comparison with Wordsworth. It is, however, a curious fact that the more one attempts to fix the similarity between the two, the more elusive does it prove to be. We might say, tentatively, that Pascoli is both more pagan and more human, notwithstanding *Margaret* and *Michael*, than Wordsworth. He is more pagan in that his delight in the beauty of a natural object is more self-sufficing, therefore more intense; it is a delight that suggests no defined religious or quasi-religious ideas, though there is always a feeling, conscious or sub-conscious, that the object is an organic part of the Universe. He is more human in that the peasants too attract him more for their own sakes than for the moral reflections to which they may give rise. They are, moreover, peasants in the full sense of the word. They are an inseparable part of their surroundings, and their interest derives from their unbroken contact with Nature, who now favours, now destroys their toil. A carefully thought out parallel study of the two poets would without doubt be interesting: it would have to set out from the fact that the fundamentals of the philosophy of the two men are essentially different: the Christianity and Platonism of the English poet being replaced in the Italian—citizen of a nation which is rapidly casting off metaphysical speculation—by a frank facing of the possibilities and probabilities opened up by modern scientific research, by a passionate longing for truth built upon the rock of scientific fact. A reference to the poet's lecture entitled *L'Era Nuova* (The New Era) will put this point beyond dispute.

Among the poems which mark most strongly this fundamental difference and this elusive similarity between Wordsworth and Pascoli is that published in the *Marzocco* of August 19th, and entitled *Inno del Mendico*. The simplicity of the diction, the spaciousness of the atmosphere, the patient resignation of the beggar-man, his harmony with the upland and the lake which form a setting for him, at once suggest Wordsworth; but the details of the poem are so totally different from any conception of Wordsworth's that a second reading shows the likeness to be superficial. Pascoli is too thoroughly modern in his scientific attitude, notwithstanding his Latin affinities (or perhaps if the matter be well thought out partly in consequence of them), to have many points of contact with any of the early Victorian English poets.

As for the *Myricæ*, the poems are so varied that it is difficult to characterise or to illustrate them. Some of the most individual and attractive —"*Dialogue*" (between sparrows and swallows), "*Hoof-beats*," and others— are very delicate word-imitations of movements, of sounds, of mental states even: and the verbal imitation is quite inseparable from the conception. The poet himself groups his little "swallow-flights of song" under a number of heads; but is nevertheless constrained to leave many standing alone. Thus we have a set of ten headed "*From Dawn to Sunset*," in which occurs the "*Hoof-beats*" already mentioned; another group entitled "*Remembrances*" in which is the little poem above quoted on the anniversary of his mother's death; another headed "*Thoughts*"—short but pregnant reflections of a philosophical character; "*Young Things*"—five tiny pieces which reveal a tender sympathy with young illusions, springing from a deep sense of the contrast between the world of the children and the reality into which they have been born. We may perhaps quote a couple as they emphasize the feeling for contrasts visible in other parts of Pascoli's work.

FIDES.

When evening was glowing all ruddy,
  and the cypresses seemed made of fine gold,
  the mother spoke to her boy-child:—
  "a whole garden's up there, made like that."
The baby sleeps and dreams of golden boughs,
  of golden trees, of forests of pure gold:
  meanwhile the cypress in the murky night
  weeps in the rainstorm, fights against the wind.

ORPHAN.

Slowly the snow falls, flake on flake:
  listen, a cradle rocks so gently.
A baby cries, with tiny thumb in mouth;
  an old dame sings with chin in hand.
The old dame sings:—"Around thy little bed
  roses and lilies grow, a lovely garden."
The baby in the cradle falls asleep:
  the snow falls slowly, flake on flake.

It will be perceived that it is not only the child in age whose illusions are touched on. The wider symbolism is at once apparent.

From the sixteen poems included in "*The Last Walk*," we may perhaps quote one that illustrates Pascoli's tendency to parable.

THE DOG.

We, while the world goes on its road

> eat out our hearts, and double is our torment,
> because it moves, because it moves so slowly.

> So, when the lumb'ring waggon passes by
> the cottage, and the heavy dray-horse
> imprints the soil with thudding hoofs,

> the dog springs from the hedgerow, swift as wind,
> runs after it, before it; whines and bays.
> The waggon has passed onward slowly, slowly;

> the dog comes sneezing back to the farm-yard.

"*In the Country*" includes eighteen charming little pieces in which the precision of the poet's wording reveals itself with striking clearness. One tiny picture we may translate. Each object in it is distinct; and a feeling of aerial perspective is given to it by the long-drawn notes of the *stornello* which are suggested at its close.

OCTOBER EVENING.

> Along the road, see, on the hedge
> laugh bunches of red berries;
> in the ploughed fields move homewards to the stall

> slowly the oxen.

> Comes down the road a beggar-man who drags
> his slow step through sharp-rustling leaves:
> in the fields a maiden raises to the wind her song:

> *Flower of the thornbush!*

Two specially charming collections occur under the heading "*Primavera*" and "*Dolcezze*." One little touch in the latter may perhaps be given.

WITH THE ANGELS.

> They were in flower, the lilacs and the olives:
> and she sat sewing at a bridal dress:
> nor had the air yet opened buds of stars,
> nor the mimosa folded yet a leaf,
> when she laughed out; yea, laughed, oh small black swallows;
> laughed suddenly. But with whom, at what?
> She laughed, so, with the angels, with those
> clouds of gold, those clouds of rose-colour.

Girls sewing or weaving, it may be remarked in passing, occur often in Pascoli's verse: one feels in them the pulse of the strong domestic affections that course through the poet's inner life.

In "*Tristezze*" Nature breathes different suggestions: it has the sweet languidness of a fine autumn day, with recollections of a gentle melancholy. A good many people have written about empty nests; but the touch, in the following quotation, of the feather on the point of being blown away, yet clinging on, is surely individual.

THE NEST.

From the wild rose-bush, just a skeleton,
there hangs a nest. How in the spring
bursts from it, filling all the air,
the twitter of the chattering housemates!

Now there's but one small feather. At the wooing
of the wind it hesitates, beats lightly;
like to some ancient dream in soul severe
that ever flies and yet is never fled.

And now the eye turns downward from the heavens—
the heavens to which one last full harmony
rose glorious, and died into the air—

and fixes on the earth, on which the leaves
lie rotting; whilst in waves the wind
weeps through the lonely country.

We must not close this most inadequate notice of the *Myricæ* without mentioning the refined tenderness of one of the closing poems, too long to quote, entitled "*Colloquio*." The poet's mother, a figure of infinite sweetness, mute and shadowy, yet real, revisits the familiar house-places with her son; and a few incidental touches put before us an idyllic sketch of the home with its plants and the two housewifely sisters, so different in character.

As a contrast to the details of the *Myricæ* we may here quote a poem that appeared (December 1897) in the *Nuova Antologia*. Breadth of silent space has as great a fascination for Pascoli as have the tender details of home and country life. He had already in one of the "*Poemetti*" dwelt with longing on the northern regions whither the wild swans fly, where the *aurora borealis* lights up the infinite polar gloom, where mountains of eternal ice rest on the sea as on a pavement; and Andrée's balloon expedition to the Pole especially fired his imagination. The poem that bears the traveller's name was written when, after long silence, there was a report that human cries had been heard on the Sofjord. In the Italian, the first part, broken by questionings and doubtings has an effect of uncertainty, like the uneasy straining of the balloon at its rope; from it the second part rises with a sure, strong leap and sinks gently at the end.

ANDRÉE.
I.

No, no. The voice borne faint athwart the gloomy
air from the realms of ice, like human cries,
was but the petrel's screech,
that loves the lonely rocks, the storms
unheard. Or maybe (was it not like children's
wailing?) maybe the sea-gull's.
A sound uplifts itself of wailful limboes
far in remotest shade untrodden:
that is the gulls, they say. Or divers, maybe?
Or the skua? Perhaps the skua—for when it flies
above the icefields, from a thousand nests
rises a strident cry; since with it draws a-near

Death's self. Or was't vain voiceless crying
in thine own heart? Nay, but the look-out heard them;
and in the look-out's ear thou trustest.
Yea, but 'twas, sure, the roar of breakers,
crashing of rocks, howling of wind, the pant
of storms far off, yet nearing,
the sky, the sea, oh Norman seafarer!

II.

Andrée was't not. Centaur, to whose swift course
the cloud is mud, the empty wind firm ground,
towards the Great Bear he flew.
Followed his flight the hornèd elks at first;
then no one more; so that there was at last
but his great heart beating above the Pole.
For he had reached the confines of the evening,
and on the Polar peak immovable
stood, as on rock black eagle.
High overhead the ocean's star burnt on
pendent, eternal lamp—
and in the lofty shadow seemed to sway.
And fixèd on his heart saw he, from this
wave, and from that, of every savage sea,
amid the calm, amid the roar of the tempest,
millions of eyes illumèd in the ray
that burned above his head; and instantly
cried he to all those eyes of that vast mirage
I reach my goal!

III.

And then, below him, solemn rose the hymn
of holy swans hyperborean; slow
and intermittent ring of unknown harps;
the knell, far off and lone amid the wind,
of bells, the closing of great gates,
hard-turning with clear clang of silver.
Nor ever sounded erst that song more loud,
more suave. They sang, that all around,
alone, pure, infinite was Death.
And o'er the wingèd man came scorn of days
that rise and fall; hatred of all the vain
outgoings that foresee the garrulous return.
High was he on the peak; with human fate
beneath him. Andrée felt himself alone,
great, monarch, God!
Now died the hymn of the sacred flock away
in tremulous trumpet blast.
Then silence. O'er the Pole the star burnt on,
like the lonely lamp of a tomb.

With the *"Poemetti,"* published in 1897, we find ourselves in the second
phase of Pascoli's work. He and his sister have left their home in S. Mauro,
with its heart-rending associations, and are settled in Barga. The trouble can
be contemplated from a distance, can be reflected upon in its general outlines,
and brought into harmony with life as a whole. But the poet's mind has not
taken refuge in the religion of the Church; he is very far from the sentiment of

Tennyson's *In Memoriam.* He finds his comfort in the delicious consciousness of quiet joy known only to those who have suffered without weakness; he finds his strength in the new perspective of life that is obtained by a fixed contemplation of the insignificant place our world holds in the Universe—of the reality of death, which for him ends all things. And this philosophy renders him very human: it focusses his affections upon his fellow mortals. Love, brotherly love, alone can keep our consciences at rest, and fully satisfy our aspirations—such is the earnest cry of this man across the threshold of whose life the hatred of a fellow man stretched the corpse of a murdered father.

The note of this philosophy is given at once in the preface of the *"Poemetti,"* addressed to his sister Maria. He gives a short indication, rather than description, of his new home with its church-towers and bells, its mountains and its rivers, its field-birds, its swallows, martins and rock-swallows, and then exclaims, addressing them:—

"Oh yes, there was a time when we did not live so near you. And if you knew what grief was ours then, what weeping, what noisy solitude, what secret and continuous anguish!"—"But come, man, think not on it," you say to me.—"Nay, let us think on it. Know that the long sweetness of your voices is born of the echoes they arouse of that past grief: that things would not be so beautiful now had they not been so black before: that I should not find so much pleasure in small motives of joy, had the suffering not been so great; had it not come from all sources of grief, from Nature and from Society; and had it not wounded me soul and body, mind and feeling. Is it not so, Maria? Blessèd, then, blessèd be grief."

And then, further on, after a charming picture of a martin that feeds, under his eaves, the abandoned nestlings of her enemy the swallow, he breaks out:—

"Men, I will speak as in a fable for children: Men, imitate that martin. Men, be content with little, and love each other within the limits of the family, of the nation, of humanity."

Twice the poet returns to the same subject. A collection of four short pieces entitled *"The Hermit,"* compact with thought, ends as follows:—

IV.

And the pale hermit veiled his eyes,
and lo throughout his heart there streamed
the sweet sleep of his weary life.
When he awoke (he was dropping
down broad, still writers in a drifting ship)
he cried: Let me remember, Lord!
God, let me dream! Nothing is more sweet,

> God, than the end of grief, but 'tis
> grievous to forget it; for 'tis hard
> to cast away the flower that only smells when plucked.

In "*The Two Children*" two little ones, having come to blows in heroic fashion at their play one evening, are ignominiously swept off to bed by their mother. In the dark, full of denser shadows, their sobbing gradually ceases, they draw nearer to each other, and when the mother comes to look at them, shading the light with her hand, she finds them pressed close together, good beyond their wont, asleep. And she tucks them in with a smile. The third part takes up the parable as follows:—

III.

> Men! in the cruel hour when the wolf is lord,
> think on the shade of destiny unknown
> that wraps us round, and on the silence awesome
>
> that reigns beyond the short noise of your brawling,
> the clamour of your warring—
> just a bee's hum within an empty hive.
>
> Peace, men! in the prone earth
> too great's the mystery, and only he
> who gets him brethren in his fear errs not.
>
> Peace, brethren! and let not the arms
> that now ye stretch, or shall, to those most near,
> know aught of strife or threat.
>
> And like good children sleeping 'twixt the sheets
> placid and white, be found,
> when unseen and unheard, above you bends
> Death, with her lighted lamp.

The poet's thought on death is given, with the insistence of one who is very much in earnest, in two recently delivered lectures, "*L'Era Nuova*," and "*La Ginestra*," ("Flower of the Broom," a development of Leopardi's exquisite poem); and again in two of his most beautiful poems, "*La Pace*" (published after the Milan riots), and "*Il Focolare*" ("*The Hearth*").

In the "*Ginestra*" Pascoli expounds Leopardi as follows:—

"And look at the stars. Reflect that there was a time when they were thought to be what they appear; small, mere atoms of light.... Instead, it is the earth that is small, a mere grain of sand. To believe the earth large and stars small; or to believe, as is the case, that the stars are infinite in number and size, and the earth very small; these are the two religions, this is the σκότος and the φῶς: darkness and light. Look at Vesuvius the destroyer, the glare of the lava glowing in the darkness. Look at Death. Look it in the face, without drooping the head cowardly, without erecting it proudly. You will feel the necessity of being at peace with your fellow-men. And say not that all men know they are mortal, but that that has never kept anyone from doing ill. I tell you it is not enough to know it; you must have your soul saturated with it, and

149

have but that in your soul. Men know, too, that the stars are large, or rather they give an idle assent to the learned who say so. They know it, that is, but they do not think it as yet. Will the time come when they will think it?" And in the "*Era Nuova*" he continues:—Man "sought illusions and found them. The brute knows not that he will die: the man said to himself that he knows he will not die. So they again came to be like each other.... And thenceforth Death being denied, no longer received from man his sad and entire assent. Man feared not to sadden his fellow, feared not to kill him, feared not to kill himself, because he no longer felt the Irreparable. I know the *Peisithanatos* (Death-persuader) who it is. I know who persuaded man to violate life in himself and in others. It is he, who, in our souls, first violated Death.... This is light. Science is beneficent in that in which she is said to have failed. She has confirmed the sanction of Death. She has sealed up the tombs again.... The proof, moved against her, is her boast. Or rather it will be when from this negation the poet-priest shall have drawn the moral essence. Who can imagine the words by which we shall feel ourselves whirling through space? by which we shall feel ourselves mortal? We know this and that: we do not feel it. The day we feel it ... we shall be better. And we shall be sadder. But do you not see that it is exactly by his sadness that man differs from the brute beasts? And that to advance in sadness is to advance in humanity?... Man, embrace your destiny! Man, resign yourself to be man! Think in your furrow, do not rave. Love—think it—is not only the sweetest but the most tremendous of actions: it is adding new fuel to the great pyre that flames in the darkness of our night."

Many will not agree with Pascoli's method of arriving at his conclusions; for men's minds are infinite in number, and but few think alike. But all will recognise the reverent earnestness of his belief, and respect the man whom hatred has moulded into a fervent apostle of love.

To understand Pascoli's power of differentiating character and handling dialogue, we must turn, not to his Italian, but to his Latin poems. These are not in any sense of the word academic exercises: they are instinct with life and of extraordinary vivacity. The crowd in which the laughing Horace finds himself wedged, in the "*Reditus Augusti*"—the poetical rivalry in the tavern between Catullus and Calvus, in the "*Catullo Calvos*"—the witty yet serious discussion between Mæcenas, Varius, Virgil and Plotius in the "*Cena in Caudiano Nervæ*"—these are charming in the extreme, and have all the piquancy of the Horatian satire. The other two poems, "*Jugurtha*" and "*Castanea*," are of a different stamp. The first is a powerful conception of the ravings and sufferings of the blinded Numidian king, in the Roman dungeon where he dies of hunger and thirst; the second is a description of the gathering and preparation of the chestnut crops, with an invocation to the tree on which alone the inhabitants of the Tuscan Apennines depend for warmth and food in winter. The peasant household is truly Virgilian in the conciseness and sympathy with which it is presented.

Truly Virgilian, too, is an Italian poem entitled "*La Sementa*" (The Sowing) published in the "*Poemetti*." There is a simple dignity in all the actions and sayings of the peasants which prevents any feeling of the triviality which the poet might so easily have suggested; prevents at the same time that sentiment of unreality which enthusiastic and romantic writers on the subject are so apt to provoke.

It is perhaps in the quiet intimateness of "*La Sementa*" that the fundamental difference between the classic inspiration of Pascoli and that of the older poet Carducci is epitomised. Carducci is a born polemist. Son of the *Risorgimento*, he passed his youth in the midst of a great epic movement, stigmatizing shams and tyrants with the resources which a wide vocabulary placed at the disposal of an exceptionally energetic and enthusiastic nature. Carducci's classicism is to a great extent formal. His verse imitates the Horatian metres, his periods are often more Latin than Italian in their construction, his women bear Latin names. And this Latin brevity, this careful exclusion of all superfluous words, this precision in the use of the smaller parts of speech (Carducci's prepositions are a study in themselves) combined with the broad imagery and ample conception that seem inseparable from the age of Garibaldi, provoke in the reader a sense of exquisite form and of impressive grandeur. The grandeur, however, sometimes degenerates into rhetoric. Pascoli is more reflective; he has more quiet sentiment. He lives in a quieter age, when the enthusiastic hopefulness of the *Risorgimento* has found its reaction in a feeling of despondency concerning the accomplished reality. He is in no sense of the word a polemist. The form of his verse and of his period is Italian, though he has, it is true, revived the Latin meaning of many Italian words. He has less grandeur than Carducci, but on the other hand he is never rhetorical. The Latin spirit has taken such complete possession of him that it has become part of himself; it leavens his whole work, but leaves it strictly individual in form and conception, and admits the expression of a sense of mystery and vagueness which is rather of the romantic than of the classic mind. As illustrative of the difference in conception between the two poets we may compare their sonnets to "*The Ox.*"

THE OX. (PASCOLI.)

> At the narrow brook, amid uncertain mists
> gazes the wide-eyed ox: in the plain
> far stretching to a sea that recedes ever,
> go the blue waters of a river:
>
> loom large before his eyes, in the misty

light, the willow and the alder;
wanders a flock upon the grass, now here now there,
and seems the herd of an ancient god.

Shadows with talons spread broad wings
in the air: mutely chimeras move
like clouds in the deep sky:

the sun goes down, immense, behind
huge mountains: already lengthen, black,
the larger shades of a much larger world.

THE OX. (CARDUCCI.)

Oh pious ox, I love thee; and a gentle feeling
of vigour and of peace thou pour'st into my heart;
whether, solemn as a monument,
thou gazest at the field so free and fruitful,

or whether, bowing gladly to the yoke,
the agile work of man thou gladly aidest;
he pricks and urges thee and thou repliest
with the slow turning of thy patient eye.

From thy broad nostril damp and dark
smokes forth thy breath, and like a joyful hymn
thy lowing rises through the quiet air;

and in the austere sweetness of thy grave
and glaucous eye, ample and quiet is reflected
the green and godlike silence of the plain.

Another side of Pascoli's mind reveals itself in his studies on Dante. The hope which *is company for me*, he writes, is to go down to posterity as an interpreter of Dante, as an illustrator of the great Poet's mind and thought. He has already published a book, *La Minerva Oscura*, for professional Dantisti; and is about to issue a series of articles for the general public.

Pascoli is now occupied on a translation, in hexameters, of the Homeric poems; and will shortly publish the glottological studies and the experiments by which he has prepared himself for his task. That he is capable of treating Greek subjects with Greek directness and simplicity, and without any affectation of Greek forms (a pitfall into which D'Annunzio continually stumbles) will be seen in the poem which closes this paper.

THE SLEEP OF ODYSSEUS.

I.

Nine days, by moon and sun, the black ship sped,
Wind-borne, helm-guided, while the creaking ropes
Were governed by Odysseus' cunning hand;
Nor—wearied—did he yield them, for the wind
Bore him on ever toward his country dear.
Nine days, by moon and sun, the black ship sped,
The hero's eye seeking unwaveringly
The rocky isle 'mid the blue-twinkling waves:
Content if, ere he died, he saw again
Its smoke-wreaths rising blue into the air.
The tenth day, where the ninth day's setting sun

Had vanished in a blinding blaze of gold,
He, peering, saw a shapeless blot of black:
Cloud was't he saw, or land? And his grave eye
Swam, conquered by the sweetness of the dawn.
Far off Odysseus' heart was rapt by sleep.

II.

And, moving towards the ship's swift flight, it seemed,
Behold a land! that nearer, nearer sailed
In misty blue, 'mid the blue-twinkling waves.
Anon a purple peak that stormed the sky;
Then down the peak the frothing gullies leaped
'mid tufts of bristling brushwood and bare rock;
And on its spurs sprang into view long rows
Of vines; and at its feet the verdant fields
Fleecy with shimmering blades of new-sprung grain,
Till it stood out entire—a rocky isle,
Harsh, and not pasture fit for neighing steed,
Altho' good nurse for oxen and wild goats.
And here and there, upon the airy peaks,
Died, in the clearness of the wakening dawn,
The herdsmen's fires: and here and there shot up
The morning swirl of smoke from Ithaca—
His home at last—! But King Odysseus' heart
Floating profound in sleep, beheld it not.

III.

And lo! upon the prow o' the hollow ship
Like angry gulls, words fly; like screaming birds
With hissing flight. The forward-straining ship
Was coasting then the high peak of The Crow
And the well-circled fount, and one could hear
The rooting of the boar-pigs; then a pen
Of ample girth appeared, with mighty rocks,
Well-builded, walled around, and hedged about
With wild-pear and with hawthorn all a-bloom.
The godlike herdsman of the boar-pigs, next,
Upon the seashore, with sharp-edgèd axe
Spoiled of its bitter bark an oakling strong,
And cut great stakes to strengthen that fair pen,
With harsh and gleaming axe-bites. Fitfully
Amid the water's wash, came o'er the sea
The hoarse pant of his strokes—that herdsman good—
Faithful Eumæus—But Odysseus' heart,
Sunk deep in slumber, heard them not at all.

IV.

And now above the ship, from prow to stern,
The sailors' furious words like arrows sped
In shuddering flight. The eager-homing ship
Abreast the harbour of Phorkyne sailed.
Ahead of it stood out the olive tree,
Large, goodly-boughed; and near to it a cave,
A cave sonorous with much-busied bees
As they in wine-bowls and in jars of stone
Perform sweet task of honey. One could see
The stony street o' the town; the houses white
Climbing the hill; distinguish, 'mid the green

Of water-loving alders, the fair fount,
The altar white, the high-raised, goodly roof—
Odysseus' high-raised steading. Now, perchance,
The shuttle whistled through the warp, and 'neath
The weary fingers grew again the web
Ample, immortal.—Yet, nor saw, nor heard
Odysseus' mighty heart, quite lost in sleep.

V.

And in the ship, now entering the port,
The worse part won the day. The men untied
The leathern bags, and straight the winds out-whistled
Furious; the sail flung wide, and flapped as doth
A peplum by a woman left outspread
To dry i' the sun upon some airy peak.
And lo! the labouring ship hath left the haven—
The haven where, upon the shore, there stood
A goodly youth propped on a spear bronze-pointed.
Under the grey-green olive stood the youth
Silent, with dreaming eyes: and a swift hound
Around him leaped, waving his plumy tail.
Now the dog checketh in his restless play
With straining eyes fixed on the infinite sea;
And, snuffing up the air o' the briny tracks,
After the flying ship he howls aloud—
Argus his dog. Yet still nor heard nor saw
Odysseus' heart, in balmy slumber bathed.

VI.

And now the ship coasted a lofty point
Of rocky Ithaca. And, twixt two hills
A garth there was, well-tilled, Laertes' field,
The ancient king's: therein an orchard rich
Where pear-trees stood, and apples, row on row,
That once Laertes gave to his dear son
Who thro' the vineyard followed, begging this
And that, among the slim new-planted trees.
Here now, ten apple-trees and thirteen pears
Stood white with blossom in a close-set clump,
And in the shade of one—the fairest—stood
An old man, turning towards the boundless sea
Where roared the sudden squall—with up-raised hand
Lessening the light above his wearied eyes—
Strained his weak gaze after the flying ship.
This was his father: but Odysseus' heart,
Floating profound in sleep, beheld him not.

VII.

And as the winds the black ship bore afar
Sudden the hero started from his sleep,
Swiftly unclosed his eyes, to see—perchance—
Smoke rise from his long-dreamed-of Ithaca—
Faithful Eumæus standing in the pen—
His white-haired father in the well-tilled field,
His father dear, who, on the mattock propped,
Stood gazing, gazing at the lessening ship—
His goodly son, who, leaning on his spear,
Stood gazing, gazing at the lessening ship—

And, leaping round his lord, with waving tail,
Argus his dog—Yea, and perchance his house,
His dear sweet home, wherein his faithful wife
Already laboured in the chattering loom.
He gazed again—a shapeless blot of black
He saw across the purpling waste of sea—
Cloud was't or land?—It faded into air
E'en as Odysseus' heart emerged from sleep.

Giovanni Pascoli's sincerity of thought, truth of feeling, breadth of sympathy, temperateness and restraint, mark him out as a poet in the full sense of the word; and place him, artistically and morally, on a higher plane than the decadents who represent Italy to the foreign public.

THE MAKING OF RELIGION

(COME SI FORMA LA RELIGIONE)

ANDREW LANG.

Longmans Green and Co.[20]

AVVERSARIO implacabile della dotta critica tedesca e degli scienziati che si rifiutino ad indagini che possano eventualmente distruggere teorie favorite, è il signor Andrew Lang. Un anno fa, egli presentò al pubblico inglese una traduzione del libro in cui il Comparetti, esaminando il poema cosiddetto epico dei Finni e le Rune delle quali il Lönnrot lo costrusse, trova parole acerbe per i Tedeschi che idearono la teoria dei *Kleine Lieder* per i poemi omerici, e che la sostennero con grande apparato scientifico basato sul nulla, per mezzo di deduzioni da ipotesi non provate, e, per la mancanza di criterii obiettivi, non dimostrabili. In un libro recente egli dà l'assalto alla teoria vigente sulle origini e sullo sviluppo della religione.

La fede in un Dio etico, onnipotente, cui non si propizia per sacrifizi di tori e di agnelli, non è un'evoluzione dall'Animismo, dall'adorazione degli antenati, che esiste tuttora fra i popoli meno progrediti, nè il concetto di un tal Dio nasce da quello astratto di spirito, come ordinariamente si asserisce. Tale fede, tale concetto si trovano fra i popoli meno evoluti che si conoscano, ma vengono sopraffatti durante il progresso materiale ed intellettuale della razza: in parte dal desiderio di avere un Dio più trattabile, meno esigente; in parte dalle invenzioni della classe sacerdotale, che per il proprio vantaggio asseconda codesto desiderio; in parte dai miti che oscurano il concetto fondamentale della Deità. Solo fra il popolo ebraico codesto concetto fondamentale potè perdurare; ma perdurò per opera dei profeti, ad onta delle tendenze popolari verso il politeismo e delle pretese della classe sacerdotale.

Tale la tesi del signor Lang. Per svilupparla, egli esamina prima le fonti da cui potrebbe scaturire, nell'uomo primitivo, l'idea di spirito; e qui non rifugge dall'investigare quelle manifestazioni della regione X della natura umana, cui gli scienziati rifiutano in generale di rivolgere l'attenzione. Il Lang è di natura alquanto scettico, ma sostiene che il consenso di tradizioni del passato di tutti i popoli e di fatti che si possono con cura verificare oggi intorno alla telepatia, alla chiaroveggenza, rende non scientifica l'attitudine di quegli scienziati i quali si rifiutano ad indagini e deridono senz'altro l'idea che esista una potenza per cui individui, senza la propria volontà o con essa, possano acquistare conoscenza di fatti accaduti, o che stanno accadendo, per altri mezzi che non siano quelli apparenti dei sensi.

Vagliando con cura le narrazioni dei viaggiatori di tutti i tempi, ma specialmente di quelli più recenti, e confrontandole colle esperienze sue proprie nell'indovinare i fatti ignoti e passati scrutando in un cristallo (*crystal-gazing, scryer*), il Lang conclude, che la chiaroveggenza, esistente in certi individui e specialmente fra certe razze (gli Scozzesi ad esempio) e molto evidentemente sviluppata (nonostante gli inganni dei "veggenti") fra i popoli meno progrediti, fornisca esperienze vere abbastanza meravigliose per dar luogo all'idea di spirito ed all'animismo che forma la religione attuale di molte tribù.

Seguendo gli ulteriori stadi dello sviluppo dell'idea religiosa, il Lang combatte fieramente lo Spencer e l'Huxley, accrescendo forza alla propria teoria con addurre fatti osservati recentemente da vari viaggiatori tra i nomadi più bassi dell'Australia, e dalla signorina Kingsley fra le tribù selvagge dell'Africa (Zulu, Bantu, ecc.). Egli prova quindi che tutte le razze primitive finora esaminate, perfino i rozzi *Bushmen* dell'Australia, hanno il concetto di un Essere onnipotente, che esisteva prima che la morte entrasse nel mondo, che vede ogni cosa, che punisce l'adulterio, la violenza alle vergini, gli assalti a tradimento non soltanto contro i componenti la stessa tribù ma anche contro altre persone. E a questo Essere non si offrono sacrifizi, perchè, secondo le parole d'un *Bushman*, "noi non gli possiamo offrir nulla che egli non abbia già."

Ora, è vero che contemporaneamente a codest'Essere concepito così largamente ed eticamente, quasi tutti i popoli adorano una folla di spiriti, che sono gli spettri di persone morte, oppure che non sono mai stati uniti ad un corpo, e che vengono propiziati con sacrifizi; di modo che il culto degli spiriti è molto più in evidenza che non quello del Dio grande e buono.

Domanda il Lang: Il Dio grande si è sviluppato più tardi da uno fra la folla degli spiriti e spettri di antenati affamati? Oppure è egli fondamentale nella religione di quei popoli? Nacque egli, per così dire, prima che, per le esperienze sopra accennate, l'idea di spirito fosse concepita; prima dunque che gli antenati e gli spiriti vaganti fossero adorati; prima che l'Animismo divenisse la religione apparente di quei popoli? L'Autore crede che quest'ultimo sia il caso. È pur difficile che lo spirito di uno stregone o di un antenato appartenente ad una sola famiglia sia stato assunto da una intiera tribù alla dignità di Essere creatore di tutto; specialmente quando si rifletta che codesti spiriti sono per lo più di indole cattiva o almeno capricciosa, che non inculcano precetti etici, e che il loro culto porge l'occasione a banchetti cari all'uomo di ogni tempo. Di più, se l'Essere creatore fosse un'evoluzione ulteriore del pensiero non più primitivo, godrebbe come prodotto recente una maggiore stima e gli sarebbe attribuita maggiore importanza che non agli altri Iddii. Invece si verifica il contrario. Il Creatore accenna fra molti popoli a sparire addirittura. Se ne parla come di un Essere misterioso, potentissimo, "di cui ci raccontavano i nostri padri," ma che è ormai quasi dimenticato. Codesto sarebbe un fatto assai strano nell'ipotesi che egli fosse un Dio più recente degli altri. Inoltre, la fede nel Creatore etico si trova con straordinaria purità fra i *Bushmen*, che non hanno il culto degli antenati; prova lampante che fra loro almeno lo sviluppo supposto dallo Spencer e dall'Huxley non ha avuto luogo.

I *Bushmen* sono nomadi. Darumulun, il Creatore etico, non ha dimora fissa, ma è da per tutto. Non avrebbe dovuto il progresso nella coltura materiale, si chiede il Lang, portare quasi logicamente un rimpiccolimento ed una conseguente degenerazione nell'idea religiosa? Le tribù nomadi prendono dimora fissa; l'Essere creatore abita, non più da per tutto, ma vicino a loro, e veglia specialmente su di loro: diviene un Dio tutelare. Le tombe dei morti, prima sparse qua e là, rimangono davanti agli occhi dei vivi; cominciano i sacrifici ai morti ed agli spiriti loro; e ne risulta un animismo fiorente accanto alla fede, mezzo dimenticata, in un Essere più grande.

E l'Animismo, domanda ancora il Lang, è valso poi a nulla nel formarsi della Religione quale l'hanno ora i cristiani? E risponde che esso, sovrapponendo la fede nella vita futura a quella nella Deità onnipotente conservataci attraverso i secoli dal popolo ebraico, ha aggiunto a questa un nuovo ed importantissimo elemento etico.

Il Vecchio Testamento accenna appena ad una vita oltretomba: il Nuovo Testamento ne parla continuamente. E gli espositori del Cristianesimo se ne valgono quale leva potentissima nello spingere il mondo lungo la strada della moralità.

Il Lang non è dogmatico. Egli rappresenta il suo libro come *la traccia di un esploratore solitario attraverso la foresta delle religioni* primitive. In ogni caso il libro merita di essere studiato: esso unisce ad una ricerca larga e coscienziosa una critica acuta, ed assale l'attuale teoria sulle origini della Religione con tanta vivacità da scuoterne fieramente le basi.

APPENDIX

APPENDIX

ADDRESSED CHIEFLY TO HER FRIENDS.

Lo Wanderer! who hast found my poor abode—
This humble rest-house for the wayfarer—
The window-flowers glow in God's sunlight dear,

The linnet's note lifteth Care's weary load,

The snowy cloth its message fair hath showed
Bidding thee freely welcome to draw near
And, glad at heart, take of my simple cheer

To help thy feet along the lonely road.

Here pause! nor lightly lift this second latch
That leadeth to the quiet inner room;

Seek not with idly curious gaze to snatch
Hints of more personal things—life's gleam or gloom;

Yet Friend! who'd know the dweller 'neath my thatch,
Enter, and mark the pattern on the loom.

(H. O. A.)

BIOGRAPHICAL NOTE

Isabella M. Anderton was born at Lower Clapton, then almost a country village, near London, in October, 1858. She was educated at Priory House School, kept by her father, where boys and girls were taught together after the manner now followed by many American schools; for Mr. Anderton, who had thought much about the theories of his work, believed strongly in such co-education. Many of his pupils, it may be said in passing (for he has now been dead some years), have justified his belief, having achieved a good measure of distinction and fame.

After matriculating at London in 1877, she went to study German for a year at Cannstadt, where she contracted a close friendship with Frau Freiligrath, wife of the German patriot-poet, whose children had also formerly been at Priory House School.

Returning to Clapton in 1878, she taught for four years in her father's school, till the weakness of her health, which she had overtaxed by the strenuousness of her work, made it imperative for her to take a rest. She therefore remained at home for a year, quietly attending lectures from Professors Burdon Sanderson and Ray Lankester, at University College.

In 1883 she went to Italy and lived for some years with a family at Genova, teaching the children and writing. Here she began those Italian studies which she pursued with such unfailing delight during the remainder of her life.

In 1887 she had another break-down, and with a friend, went up to the Apennines above Pistoia to recruit. Here, however—at Prunetta—her illness became so serious that, in response to a telegram, a brother and sister hurried out to her assistance. On their arrival a move was made to Cutigliano, where she slowly recovered strength. During this visit to the Pistoiese she came closely into touch with the peasants of the neighbourhood, studying their folk-lore and their ways of thought with keen and sympathetic interest. Her exceptional knowledge of Italian, and her instinct for the genius of the race, enabled her to go with a rare directness home to the minds and affections of her peasant-friends; and, of the literary results—The Tuscan Stories and Sketches here given—a considerable number were contributed to "Good Words."

After this she left the family with whom she had been living, but remained in Genova, teaching and writing, till her marriage in October, 1890, to Rodolfo Debarbieri, when they removed to Florence, in which fascinating city the remainder of her life was spent, in the heart of its literary and artistic life. Here their only child, a son, was born in 1891; and in course of time it was arranged that this son should be sent to receive his education in England.

In 1899 she was appointed to the English Chair in the Istituto SS. Annunziata, where her work and influence over the pupils were highly valued by all, not only for their intellectual but also for their stimulating moral qualities.

In 1900 she had to undergo a serious operation, most skilfully performed by Professor Colzi of Florence. This, though successful for the time, seems to have left a legacy of evil, and in 1902 a further operation became necessary. She continued her work, however, bravely once more, writing on literary and artistic subjects with unfailing zest, and in June, 1904, seemed to her friends to have completely recovered her health and strength. But the final blow fell swiftly. In July illness seized her again, and carried her off in the December following, after terrible sufferings borne with a fortitude which one can hardly call other than heroic. No thanks can be adequate for the care and kindness of her friend Dr. Oscar Marchetti, who could not have done more for her had she been his own sister; nor for the whole-hearted devotion of her maid Paolina.

She was followed by a distinguished company of friends, fellow-professors, and artists, to the Protestant cemetery of the Allori, about a mile and a half outside the Porta Romana—a peaceful enclosure, with its solemn cypresses and weeping ashes, set like an island amid the sunny olive-clad hills she loved so well. Here, at the foot of an avenue of cypresses, she was laid to rest; and thus the sentiment of the prose-poem given in this volume seems to cling about her to the end.

Her command of Italian and knowledge of the literature were extraordinary; and in fact she was often taken during later years for an Italian, on one occasion asking a friend rather ruefully if it were true that she spoke English with an accent: and, by living with Italians of all classes, she obtained an understanding of their habits of thought and more intimate life that few foreigners possess. French and German, too, were at command, as well as Latin, and to a less extent Greek; one of her most valuable works being a study of the character of Virgil's Dido, especially interesting as being from a woman's point of view. It is much to be regretted that this cannot now be traced, or it would have been included here. She undertook for Senatore Domenico Comparetti the translation into English of his "*Traditional Poetry of the Finns*" (1898), and had many an interesting discussion with him as to the manner of its English presentment. At first he was rather inclined to resent her vigorous pruning of his elaborate periods, though in the end he saw that, though admissible in Italian, they were impossible in English. Indeed a few months ago he said with picturesque Italian politeness that he had come to prefer the translation to the original. This translation, with a preface by Mr. Andrew Lang, was published by Messrs. Longmans in 1898. For about ten years she was Florence correspondent to The Studio, her chief contributions being *Pietro Fragiacomo* (Oct. 1899): and *Domenico Morelli* (Nov. 1901). These articles she wrote, as was always her custom, under her maiden name.

Her work on literature and art gave her the keenest delight, as also did the beauty of the city of Florence and her friendship with some of its most interesting residents. The fascination too of the Tuscan hills and plains appealed deeply to her, as did the romance of Elba where she once went for a long holiday with her brother. Rome, Venice, Siena, and the varied beauties of Italy—perhaps these appealed to her the more poignantly that her physical wellbeing seemed gradually more precarious and elusive. Latterly it was a long war between her will and her weakness; between the *vivida vis animi*—the living force of her indomitable spirit—and the *ineluctabile fatum*—the fate whose grip none may escape. Yet with unquenched hope she struggled on, keeping for her friends a cheerful sunniness, and for those in need of help and comfort a well-spring of encouragement. If the motto she once adopted:
—

Ad Augusta per Angusta,

was not realised in a material sense, it may stand, as inscribed on the marble in the Allori, as symbolical of a spiritual struggle and attainment.

The singular combination in her nature of English and Italian characteristics is well expressed in the beautiful words of her friend the poet Angiolo Orvieto, writing just after her death in the Florentine literary paper "*Il Marzocco*":—

"Isabella M. Anderton.—È morta a Firenze, ove abitava da parecchi anni, la signora Isabella M. Anderton, elegante e dotta scrittrice di arte italiana su parecchie riviste inglesi tra le quali *The Studio*. Esperta della lingua e della letteratura nostra, fece inglesi con efficacia e fedeltà prose e poesie: e son degne di speciale ricordo le sue versioni dal Pascoli—di cui era ammiratrice ed amica—e la traduzione del *Kalevala* di Domenico Comparetti.—Venuta dall'Inghilterra in Italia, ella contemperò in una incantevole armonia le energiche virtú della sua stirpe e le grazie della nostra. Fu inglese nella operosa tenacia del volere, nella tempra metallica del carattere; italiana nell'elegante agilità dello spirito, nella sensibilità vivida e pronta, nella fantasia colorita. Fu donna nel senso più delicato di questa parola e nel senso più alto; e seppe mostrare alla sventura un volto sorridente. Insegnante valentissima, ebbe la cattedra di lingua inglese al Collegio dell'Annunziata e seppe cattivarsi l'affetto e la stima delle sue allieve, che ricorrevano a lei per consiglio ed aiuto anche dopo lasciata la scuola. Il *Marzocco*, che ne ebbe qualche volta la collaborazione, si unisce ai molti che in Firenze e fuori ne piangono la scomparsa."

"There has passed away at Florence, where she had lived many years, Isabella M. Anderton, an elegant and learned writer on Italian art in several English reviews, among them THE STUDIO. *Well skilled in our language and literature, she turned both prose and verse into strong and faithful English: worthy of special mention being her versions of Pascoli—of whom she was an admirer and friend—and her translation of the* KALEVALA *of Domenico Comparetti. An Englishwoman settled in Italy, she blended in an enchanting harmony the nervous energy of her race and the grace of ours. She was English in her energetic tenacity of will, finely tempered as a blade of steel; Italian in her agile grace of spirit, in her vivid and ready sensibility, in the glowing colours of her imagination. She was a woman in the truest and highest sense of the word; and knew how to meet adversity with a smiling face. A most excellent teacher, she held the Chair of English Letters at the Collegio dell'Annunziata, where she fairly captivated the affections and esteem of her pupils who went to her for counsel and advice after having left the school. The* MARZOCCO, *to which she was a contributor, joins with many in Florence and elsewhere in mourning her loss."*

9 783734 080845